Leigh Egerton

Ballads and Legends of Cheshire

Leigh Egerton

Ballads and Legends of Cheshire

ISBN/EAN: 9783742899927

Manufactured in Europe, USA, Canada, Australia, Japa

Cover: Foto ©Andreas Hilbeck / pixelio.de

Manufactured and distributed by brebook publishing software
(www.brebook.com)

Leigh Egerton

Ballads and Legends of Cheshire

BALLADS
&
LEGENDS
of
Cheshire
LONGMANS & CO
LONDON.
1867

Dedicated

TO

THE MOST NOBLE

THE MARQUIS OF WESTMINSTER, K.G.

ONE OF CHESHIRE'S BEST FRIENDS.

PREFACE.

LORD RANDAL, the great enemy of Llewellyn, found himself one day surprised, in his castle of Rothlent, in Flintshire, by a very superior force; he sent an express to his great general, Roger Lacy, Constable of Chester, desiring immediate relief. This express found Lacy at Chester, during the anniversary of the Midsummer fair. The occasion was urgent, and the general, we conclude, having no regular force at his disposal, marched immediately to the relief of Earl Randal with a *vast* (as we should say in Cheshire) of players, fiddlers, musicians, minstrels, and any other vagabonds he could assemble, whom chance had drawn to the same focus by the loadstone of the fair. Llewellyn, alarmed at the approach of this multitude, raised the siege with the utmost precipitation. When Earl Randal's triumphant cavalcade made its public entry into Chester, after their success in forcing Llewellyn to raise the siege, it is most probable that the victorious minstrels played before the Earl; and it is known that the minstrels (at the annual feast kept on the Midsummer commemoration of the anniversary of the day) always headed the procession to St. John's Church, playing on their instruments before the Lord of Dutton, the Earl of Chester's representative, to whom the Constable's son, John Lacy, had transferred the minstrel prerogative given by Earl Randal to his father, with other rights and privileges, upon his return to Chester after his rescue from Llewellyn. The father of this Rafe Dutton is supposed to have marched at the head of the band of minstrels, against Llewellyn, as mentioned above. The anniversary of the solemnity was celebrated on the festival of John the Baptist, by a procession of all the minstrels to the church dedicated to this tutelary Saint in the city of Chester. After having been constantly observed for at least five hundred and fifty years, the procession seems to have been discontinued A.D. 1758, about a century since.

To prove how some exclusive privileges (of which the licensing minstrels granted by our Cheshire monarch was one) were respected by the legislature, we find that the Act 29 of Elizabeth, which declares all itinerant minstrels to be vagabonds, particularly excepts the minstrel jurisdiction of John Dutton, of Dutton in Cheshire, Esquire. It was not, then, very unnatural for me to suppose that Cheshire (the former abode, and latest stronghold, of the minstrels of England) would be especially rich in the songs, ballads, and relics of minstrels and minstrelsy, beyond any other county. The result, however (as far as my own inquiries have extended), has not justified nor realised my anticipations. In my small collection I have not been able to include a single specimen that I can positively assert to be a remnant of the legitimate minstrels of Cheshire; and with the exception of Geoffrey Whitney, Broome, and Parnell, I know of no Cheshire-born poets of the past age; for Reginald Heber, though gone, can hardly yet rank with the past, nor like Rowland Warburton with the present age. I have seen many election squibs, personalities, &c., of auld lang syne, but have reproduced none of them; for if there is one thing more than another ephemeral, and incomprehensible and uninteresting even to the next generation, it is an election squib. Like a rocket or shell, its one discharge may have been fatal, but it is innocuous ever afterwards, and the débris not worth collecting.

I have avoided almost all topographical descriptions, which are generally uninteresting to the mind, however the sight of the beauties of nature may delight and charm the eye. I have steered clear of prologues, epilogues, laments, and elegies; I have transcribed but few epitaphs; I have rigorously excluded first views, farewells, *et hoc genus omne.* My history may be proved faulty. I am aware, for instance, that, according to Hume, Edward I. on his return from the Holy Land, after hearing of his father's death at Sicily, landed in France before visiting England. I have only made him do what he ought to have done—namely, go home first; and Grafton, in his Chronicle, corroborates my version. 'Wherefore in all hast he (Edward I.) sped him into England, and came to London the seconde of August,' &c.

Sir Walter Scott observed to a friend who pointed out to him an inaccuracy in his 'Bonnets of Bonny Dundee,' 'We cannot always be particular in a ballad.' It may be alleged of one of the ballads written by my talented friend Mr. John Leigh, 'The Knight's Lowe and Lady's Grave,' that Sir Piers Legh (of Agincourt fame) is buried at Macclesfield; but who shall say that he was not first buried on Knight's Lowe? It is difficult to prove a negative, and great people's remains in former times were buried piecemeal in different places. Canova, all the dismembered saints (and quite recently the late King of Prussia), are examples of this. Grafton, in his Chronicle, in speaking of Richard I. says: 'He was buried, as he himself willed, at Everard, at the feet of his father; howbeit his hart was buried at Roen, and his Bowelles at Poytiers.'

If I have been disappointed in not having met any minstrel relics, I have been equally so in the paucity of our legends; but Cheshire, generally speaking, is a flat county, and the ideal flourishes most amongst mountains and streams; and few even of our many castles and sites of castles have any extant traditionary lore attached to them, or it would long since have been unearthed by Mr. Beamont, or some other of our zealous county antiquaries. I have been in correspondence, in the course of my inquiries after the past, with many gentlemen and antiquaries, from all of whom I have met undeviating kindness; and if I have in a great degree been unsuccessful in my researches, I believe that the actual non-existence, or I may rather say disappearance, of material has been the cause of failure.

A long hiatus elapsed between the invention of printing and the energetic pursuit of antiquarian lore. Printing put an end to the story-teller's occupation; but at the time the live books were discarded, the new art did not, whilst there was yet time, collect the stories of oral tradition, and the treasures of auld lang syne, and preserve and pot them for posterity. Wherever I have found anything that suited my purpose, I have copied it—like 'The Old Man outwitted,' and other extracts, from 'Halliwell's Palatine Anthology.' Halliwell was himself disappointed at the poverty of materials for his work. I have strictly kept to Cheshire. Had I travelled to Derbyshire, Lancashire, and other adjacent counties, my field of material would at once have extended itself, but my object has been to collect a 'Cheshire Garland' purely and solely. Should this collection be the means of eliciting any hitherto concealed broadsides, or bringing from their dusty retreat any black letter curiosities or manuscript legends and ballads relating to Cheshire, my trouble, or rather my amusement, may not be thrown away. I may be the jackal to some future antiquarian lion, and I may be the means of putting into the heads of efficient men the idea of collecting the ballads, legends, and odds and ends of the past, belonging to their respective counties, before the wave of oblivion closes over the fast disappearing materials. I have rejected some able articles on Cheshire, the source of which was entirely owing to the imagination, and not to *some*, however faint, traditional foundation, or which might well from their length be published alone. I believe, such as it is, it is the only attempt to collect and publish an *olla podrida* about Cheshire that has been made; and I may say to any reader—

> Si quid novisti rectius istis,
> Candidus imperti ; si non, his utere mecum.

EGERTON LEIGH.

The West Hall, High Leigh:
August 1866.

CONTENTS.

Contents.

Contents. xvii

Contents.

LIST OF ILLUSTRATIONS.

Cheshire

LEGENDS, BALLADS, &c.

Legend of the *Constable Sands*.

[Taken from the 'Life of St. Werburghe,' translated by Henry Bradsha (Bradshaw), a Benedictine monk of St. Werburgh's Monastery in Chester, who died 1513. The 'Life of St. Werburghe' was printed first in London in 1521 (Black Letter); of this edition only five copies are known to be extant. It was reprinted by the Chetham Society, 1848.

It seems the Abbey of Norton was founded by William Fitznigell (the son of Nigel), Baron of Haulton, in the year 1210. The date of the legendary miracle would probably be a short time previous to that year.

Throughout the poem, to produce anything like rhythmical intonation, the stress must be laid on the last syllable of each line, utterly irrespective of sense.]

Howe sondes rose up within the salt see agaynst Hilburghee *by* Saynt Werburge, *at the peticion of the Constable of* Chestre.

THE seconde Erle of *Chestre* after the Conquest
Was Erle *Richard*, son to *Hug. Lupus*,
Whiche *Richarde* entended all thyng to the best,
To visite Saynt *Winifrede* in hert desirous,
Upon his journey went, myn auctour sayth thus,
Devoutly to holy well in pylgrimage,
For his great merite and gostly advantage.

Whan the wicked *Walshemen* herd of his comyng
After a meke maner unto that party,
They made insurrection inwardly gladdyng ;
Descended from the mountaynes most furiously,
Agaynst the erle raised a cruell company,
Bytwxt hym and *Chestre* lettynge the kyngis way,
Purposynge to slee or take hym for a praye.

The erle son perceyved theyr malicious entent,
In all hast possible sende to *Chestre* secretly,
To warne his constable by love and commandment,
Wyllyam the son of *Nigell*, to rayse a great army
To mete hym at *Basyngwerke* right sone and spedely,
For his deliveraunce from deth and captivite
Of the wyld *Walshemen*, without humanite.

The constable congregate in all goodly hast
A myhty strong host, in theyr best arraye,
Toward *Hilburghee* on journey ridyng fast,
Trustyng upon shippes all them to convaye,
Whiche was a riall rode that tyme, nyght and daye ;
And whan they theder came, shyppyng none there was
To carie all them over in convenient space.

Alas ! what hert may thynke, or tonge well expresse,
The dolorous grevaunce and great lamentacion
That the host made, for love and tendernes,
Knowynge their great maister in suche persecucion ?
Some wept and wayled without consolacion,
Some sighed and sobbed, some were in extasy
Without perfect reason.   Alas ! what remedy ?

Wyllyam the constable, most carefull man on lyve,
Of his mysfortune in suche extreme necessite
Called to hym a monke there dwellyng contemplatyve,
Required hym for counsayle and prayer for his charite.
The monke exhorted hym to knele upon his kne,
Humblie to beseke *Werburge* his patronesse
For helpe and remedy in suche great distresse.

The constable content, anone began to praye :
' O blessed *Werburge* and virgin pure,
I beseke the mekely helpe me this day,
That we may transcende this ryver safe and sure,
To save and defende my lord from discomfiture ;
And here I promytte to *God*, and the alone,
To offre to the a gyfte at my comyng whome.'

Whyche prayer ended with wepyng and langour,
Beholde and consydre well with your gostly ee
The infinite goodness of our *Saviour* ;
For like as to *Moises* devided the *Redde See*,
And the water of *Jordan* obeyed to *Josue*,
Ryht so the depe river of *Dee* made division,
The sondes drye appered in syght of them echone.

The constable consyderynge and all the company
This great myracle transcendyng nature,
Praysed and magnified our Lorde *God Almygty*,
And blessed *Werburge*, the virgin pure.
They went into *Wales* upon the sondes sure,
Delivered their lorde from drede and enmite,
Brought hym in safe garde agayne to *Chestre* cite.

The sayd *Wyllyam* constable came to the monasterye,
Thanked Saynt *Werburge* with meke supplicacion,
Fulfylled his promes made in extremite,
Offred to the place the village of *Neuton*.
Afterwarde he founded the abbay of *Norton*,
And where the host passed over betwix bondes
To this day ben called the *Constable Sondes*.

The *Constable Sands*.

A slightly different Version from the preceding Legend.

PART I.

HE Earl of *Chester* a pilgrimage went,—
   For he had vowed a dole
   For the good of his soul,—
To St. *Winifred*'s well his steps he bent.

Whilst prostrate at *Winifred*'s shrine he lay,
   Confessed that the devil,
   The father of evil,
Had tempted him sore for many a day ;

Contrite resolved he would never again
   Do a thing that was wrong—
   That his life might last long—
Nor wilfully break even one of the Ten.

But suddenly roused, he sprang to his feet;
   For his henchman appeared,
   And said that he feared
A body of Welsh knaves, who filled the street,

Were coming a prisoner the Earl to make :
  Finding he was alone,
  Or at most with but one,
Was too good a chance for them not to take.

PART II.

Lord *Richard* turned, and daring fate,
  His trusty falchion drew ;
To *Basingwerks*, near abbey gate,
  With lightning speed he flew.

Yelled on the view the robber pack,
  And four before the rest,
Pursuing hotly on his track,
  Behind his footsteps prest.

Earl *Richard* thundered at the gate,
  And loud he blew his horn ;
Up rushed the four, impelled by hate,
  Before the bolts were drawn.

Through one the Earl his vengeful sword
  (As raised his arm) he drove ;
The henchman, fighting near his lord,
  Another's headpiece clove.

The third rushed up ; the Earl his hand
  Lopped off by backward blow ;
The fourth drew back until his band
  Should join to crush their foe.

The Earl and henchman passed the gate
  As the mad host foamed near :
A moment more—they'd been too late
  The abbey's porch to clear.

(The Lord of *Hatton*, cross the *Dee*,
  Was waiting for the Earl ;
The trustiest constable was he
  Who did a flag unfurl.)

As the *Welsh* thundered at the door,
  Like she-wolf robbed of whelp,
The Earl with grief the flood-tide saw
  That severed him from help.

The *Welsh* too see the flowing tide
  Rolled deep before their foe ;
No timely aid from *Cheshire* side
  Can come across they know.

The Earl spread signals to the breeze,
  To show he was betrayed,
Then to St. *Werburgh* on his knees
  Thus help and mercy prayed :—

PRAYER.

'Holy St. *Werburgh*,
In danger to thee,
Pressed hard by robbers,
For refuge I flee.

Thou canst show a way
E'en o'er the deep wave :
Without thee I die,
Thy suppliant save !
Hear now but my prayer,
An abbey I'll found,
Where monks through all time
Thy praises shall sound.'

PART III.

Scarce had he ceased, when, raised from *Deva*'s flood,
  A solid ledge of sand,
  Raised by St. *Werburgh*'s hand,
Dry midst the waters like a stone wall stood ;

Stretched from the Cambrian to *Cheshire* shore,
  As when the *Red Sea* gaped
  For *Jews* from *Egypt* 'scaped,
When stiffened paused the waves' mighty roar.

Up rose in haste the Lord of *Hatton*'s men,
  And soon that *Cheshire* host
  The holy bridge had crost.
Panicstruck fled the Welsh freebooters then.

Earl *Richard* 's saved !—and from that hour far famed
  St. *Werburgh*'s Bridge of Sand,
  Reared by his saintly hand,
Has *Constable Sands* been most rightly named.

The Spanish Lady's Love.

WILL you hear a Spanish ladye,
    How she wooed an English man ?
Garments gay and rich as may be,
    Decked with jewels, she had on.
Of a comely countenance and grace was she,
And by birth and parentage of high degree.

    As his prisoner there he kept her—
        In his hands her life did lye—
    Cupid's bands did tie them faster
        By the liking of an eye.
In his courteous company was all her joy ;
To favour him in anything she was not coy.

    But at last there came commandment
        For to set the ladies free,
With their jewels still adorned,
        None to do them injury.
Then said the lady mild, ' Full woe is me ;
Oh, let me still sustain this kind captivity !

'Gallant captain, show some pity
    To a lady in distress ;
Leave me not within the city
    For to die in heavinesse.
Thou hast this present day my body free,
But my heart in prison still remains with thee.'

HE.

' How shouldst thou, fair lady, love me,
    Whom thou knowst thy country's foe ?
Thy fair words make me suspect thee :
    Serpents lie where flowers grow.'

SHE.

' All the harm I wish to thee, most courteous knight,
God grant the same upon my head may fully light.

' Blest be the time and season
    That thou cam'st on Spanish ground ;
If our foes you may be termed,
    Gentle foes we have you found.
With our cytye, you have won our hearts each one ;
Then to your country bear away what is your owne.'

HE.

' Rest you still, most gallant ladye,
    Rest you still, and weep no more ;
Of fair lovers there are plenty—
    Spain doth yield a wondrous store.
Spaniards fraught with jealousy we often find,
But *Englishmen* through all the world are counted kind.'

SHE.

'Leave me not unto a *Spaniard*;
    You alone enjoy my heart.
I am lovely, young, and tender;
    Love is likewise my desert.
Still to serve thee day and night my heart is prest :
The wife of every *Englishman* is counted blest.'

HE.

' 'T would be a shame, fair ladye,
    For to bear a woman hence ;
English soldiers never carry
    Any such without offence.'

SHE.

' Ill quickly change myself, if this be so,
And like a page I'll follow thee where'er you go.'

HE.

' I have neither gold nor silver
    To maintain thee in this case ;
And to travel is great charges,
    As you know, in every place.'

SHE.

' My chains and jewels every one shall be thine own,
And eke five hundred pounds in gold that lies unknown.'

HE.

'On the seas are many dangers,
    Many storms do there arise ;
Which will be to ladies dreadful,
    And force tears from their bright eyes.'

SHE.

'Well, in troth, I should endure extremite,
For I could find in heart to lose my life for thee.'

HE.

'Courteous ladye, leave this fancie,
    Here comes all that breeds the strife,—
I in *England* have already
    A sweet woman to my wife.
I will not falsify my vow for gold nor gain,
Nor yet for all the fairest dames that live in *Spain.*'

SHE.

'Ah ! how happy is that woman
    Who enjoys so true a friend !
Many happy days *God* send her—
    Of my suit I make an end.
On my knees I pardon crave for my offence,
Which did from love and true affection first commence.

'Commend me to thy lovelie ladye,
    Bear to her this chain of gold,
And these bracelets for a token,
    Grieving that I was so bold.

All my jewels in like sort take thou with thee,
For they are fitting for thy wife, and not for me.

'I will spend my days in prayer,
  Love and all her wiles defye ;
In a nunnery I will shroud me,
  Far from any companye.
But e'er my prayers do end, be sure of this,
To pray for thee and for thy love I will not miss.

'Thus farewell, most gallant captain !
  Farewell, too, my heart's content !
Count not Spanish ladies wanton,
  Though to thee my love was bent.
Joye and true prosperite go ever with thee !'

HE.

'The lyke fall ever to thy share, most faire ladye !'

Sir Uryan Legh (the Spanish Ladye's lover?) was the son of Thomas Legh of Adlington, and was knighted by the Earl of Essex at the siege of Cadiz (Sept. 1596). It was during this expedition he was said to have been engaged in the adventure which gave rise to the ballad. The original portrait of Sir Uryan Legh, in a Spanish dress, still exists at Bramhall (Colonel Davenport's old hall). Sir Uryan was High Sheriff of Cheshire, A.D. 1613.

THE SPANISH LADY.

The Spanish Lady.

Cheshire Cavalry.

[Composed whilst at Liverpool by John Hayward, of Stamford Bridge,
private in the Forest Troop.]

COME, all you British heroes, and listen to my song,
    To these few lines I here have penned ; they won't
        detain you long.
    It's concerning of the yeomanry regimental orders
        —they
Who marched into *Liverpool* on the twenty-eighth of *May.*

CHORUS.

So let the trumpet sound as we march along the way ;
And we marched into *Liverpool* on the twenty-eighth of *May*,
And we marched into *Liverpool* all on a *Saturday.*

The *Cheshire* Yeoman Cavalry are men of high renown,
Give credit to their country and honour to their crown ;
When mounted on their warlike steeds to *Liverpool* we'll go,
Along with Colonel *Egerton*, that valiant hero.

And when the time does come our country for to leave,
Behold our wives and sweethearts, how they lament and grieve !
' Good by, my loving daddy ! '—this is the children's cries :
Their mothers they receive them with tears in their eyes.

Behold our loving sweethearts, they know not what to do;
But soldiers they prove loyal, constant, and true.
We give to them a loving kiss : 'Farewell, love ; don't complain,
And I will marry you, my dear, when I return again.'

Sir *Philip* is our captain, at *Oulton* he doth dwell ;
We thank him for his kind treat—the truth I do tell ;
With roast beef and plum-pudding, and everything at large,
On the north shore at *Liverpool* he led us to the charge.

There is Lieutenant *Palin*, a-mounted on his grey,
And when he draws his broadsword, he boldly clears the way ;
Likewise Cornet *Potts*—he is both straight and tall ;
He 's willing for to serve the Queen, when on him she doth call.

There is Captain *Hill*, our adjutant, a hero bold you know ;
He boldly fought at *Waterloo*, and faced the daring foe ;
He boldly fought with sword in hand till victory was won,
He let that tyrant for to know he was true *Britain*'s son.

There is Quartermaster *Oulton* ; he ordered in our corn—
He is a noble forester, for in it he was born ;
He saw us righted in our weight, I will make bold to say,
When we arrived at *Liverpool* on the twenty-eighth of *May*.

There is Sergeant-Major *Walker*—the truth I do tell ;
He boldly fought at *Waterloo*, where many thousands fell.
He says, ' My boys, be steady !--you can if you will.'
On *Monday* we expected to have a heavy drill.

The composer of this song rides Mr. *Palin*'s grey ;
'Twas in the year forty-one from the ranks he broke away.
The troopers they would have laughed ; but, fear they should be
     fined,
Says Corporal *Jenkins*, 'There he goes, and leaves them all
     behind.'

Now let a health go round : let's drink to our Queen ;
The second to our Colonel, a bumper to the brim ;
The third to all our officers, in station what they be ;
The fourth unto the *Cheshire* lads—they'll fight for liberty.

So now my song is ended ; I hope it proves in rhyme ;
I might it much amended, if I had a little time ;
I might it much amended, but being near noon,
So we marched out of *Liverpool*, all on the fourth of *June*.

CHORUS.

So let the trumpets sound a merry, merry tune,
As we march out of *Liverpool*, all on the fourth of *June*.

The Earl of Chester's Yeomanry Cavalry, till of late years, used always to meet at Liverpool, not at Chester, as at present.

Legend of *Chester*.

'When the daughter is stolen shut the Pepper Gate.'—*Old Cheshire Proverb.*

PART I.

THERE was a mayor's daughter in *Chester's* old town
The fairest of maidens who e'er donned a gown ;
Her father's sole child—save her he had none.
When he kissed her fair brow, he ne'er sighed for a
But somehow he forgot that a maid of eighteen   [son,
Is grown up; for fathers don't think oft, I ween,
That the time steals on fast when young girls, 'tis feared,
Are wont to change dolls for a man with a beard.
And his friends used to say, when they saw her wild ways,
' Ah ! she'll give him the slip one of these fine days.'
Oh ! how lovely she was ! her skin was as fair
As the flowers in the *Kailyards*, that garland the pear ;
Her voice soft and clear as a musical bell,
Though on many ears of her lovers it fell
As the note of despair, and their fondest hope's knell.
No youth who'd e'er gazed on her face, you'd suppose,
Had ever before seen a maiden like *Rose* ;
She charmed all, at once : 'twas not only her face,
But a certain most indescribable grace ;

WHEN THE DAUGHTER IS STOLEN, SHUT THE PEPPER GATE.

A ' je ne sais quoi,' as the *Frenchman* would say,
Which in spite of themselves stole all hearts away.
Her long curling tresses, though dark as the night,
When kissed by the sunbeam shone golden with light.
Her eyes of that sort, should she once glance at you,
You'd for ever to all peace of mind bid adieu;
You'd fancy all day you felt those flashing eyes ;
In dreams those same looks would your pillow surprise.
She was not that species of daughter you see,
Whom parents dare hope long for them would make tea.
She'd a will of her own ; and t'was whispered about,
There was one of her lovers whom she did not flout.
A certain Welsh knight, with a long pedigree,
Was often seen crossing the bridge o'er the *Dee*.
The *Chester* old ladies declared he was poor;
This might be scan. mag. that was laid at his door:
But whatever might be the state of his *purse*,
His *person* the lady liked never the worse.
He was not the man to whom fair maids might say
That most disagreeable of short words, called Nay.
Young, noble, and handsome, a devil-may-care,
With the brain to conceive, and the brave heart to dare ;
Amongst men, a lion ; with ladies, a lamb ;
A look that said, laughing, ' Refuse me who can ? '
Deeds fullest of danger he loved most to face ;
(As surgeons gloat over some desperate case).
Woman's weakness makes woman delight in the strong,
The fairest thus 'tis to the bravest belong.
Rose's father (whose wealth and estates were untold)
Hated penniless sons-in-law ; would have looked cold
On lover half *Bayard*, half *Solomon*, who

Might be an *Apollo* and *Hercules* too,
Should he, without gold, dare his daughter to woo ;
And perhaps have preferred a *rich* chieftain of cowards
To a *poor* man whose veins boiled with blood of the *Howards*.
It is lucky for some men, if not for the fair,
Papas don't choose always for daughters a pair.

PART II.

Merrily smiled the dewy morn,
  Sparkled with gems the Dee ;
Near Pepper Gate rang out a horn,
  It sounded cheerily.

Rose and young friends are met to play,
And while the sunny hours away.
Hither and thither flies the ball;
Maidens on maidens blithely call,
Chasing the orb through *Pepper Street*
With waving hands and bounding feet.

Merrily smiled the dewy morn,
  Sparkled with gems the Dee ;
Near Pepper Gate rang out a horn,
  It sounded cheerily.

Backwards and forwards bounds the ball,
Pursued by nymphs it leaps the wall ;
Through *Pepper Gate* in crowds they run ;
Back to the street the ball is flung ;
Hotter and hotter grows the fun.

PART III.

Where's *Rose*?　Her comrades turn and look,
As when *Pluto Proserpine* took
To shades below with his four-in-hand,
When she strayed lost in flowery land;
For there was *Rose* en croupe behind
The young Welsh knight, nor looked unkind.
No rose (they say) but has a thorn.
He looked as smiling as the morn,
Howe'er that be, and blew his horn.
His charger prancing o'er the *Dee*,
The weight unfelt, aghast they see.
Knight and lady were out of sight;
Echo of hoofs was silent quite;
Yet gazed her friends like startled deer:
Their thoughts I know not, but I fear
That on love-subjects maids oft are
Antagonistic to papa.
At length all 'gan at once to talk
(A real lapsus linguarum) lauk
Our *Chester* damsels set at naught
The law in some Scotch household taught.
This was the rule—' That at *one* time
No more should speak than women *nine*.'
' Why, *Rose* is off ! '—' *I* always said
In reg'lar way she'd never wed.'—

‘ She’ll lead them a terrible dance.’—
‘ There’s an end to my brother’s chance.’—
‘ Oh, what a bore ! she always said
That I should be her first bridesmaid.’—
‘ Dear me, what a goose ! she’ll have no trousseau.’—
‘ I wonder how ever she could do so.’—
‘ He’s very good-looking.’—‘ And a knight.’—
‘ He’s as poor as *Job*.’—‘ They’re out of sight.’—
‘ My dear, he springs from gentle blood.’—
‘ Those heiresses ne’er come to good ! ’—
‘ Heiress ! her chance of fortune’s small.’—
‘ I don’t agree with you at all.’—
‘ I’d run away myself.’—‘ For shame ! ’—
‘ Then he has *such* a pretty name ! ’—
‘ Who’ll get the gowns she’s left behind ? ’—
‘ Will her father be long unkind ? ’—
‘ He will.’—‘ He won’t.’—‘ She’ll on her knees
Say, Father, kiss your *Rosy*, please.’—
‘ All be forgiven and forgot.’—
‘ You don’t know what a sire she’s got.’—
‘ I saw the knight give *Rose* a kiss.’—
‘ How far d’ye think they’ve got by this ? ’—
‘ Oh ! she was merry as a lark.’—
‘ How *John* admired her tresses dark ! ’—
‘ Should you call her so *very* fair ? ’—
‘ Dear me ! who will dress her back hair ? ’—
‘ I wonder, when they come back here,
If my mamma will call on her ? ’—
‘ They say he’s wild as mountain hawk.’—
‘ My word, there’ll be a pretty talk.’—

' Which of us dare her father tell
That his loved *Rose,* our *Chester* belle,
Is o'er the hills and far away ?
Stormy end to our sunny day.'—
Bad news flies fast, and *Chester*'s mayor
At once began his locks to tear,
Bustled for nothing here and there.
Oh ! how he blest that *Lochinvar* !
Swore his daughter he'd ne'er forgive !
Vowed her lover should never live !
Declared his wealth he'd leave the poor,
Nor *Rose* should *never* cross his door.
He summoned his friends.   Say what to do?
Was it the fond pair to pursue ?
No, neither he nor friends could ride,
And no horses had they beside,
To bring back *Rose* a contrite nun
Before the words could be said or sung
That makes at once of two hearts one.
Did he call out the archer guard
To stop the knight with swift cloth-yard ?
No—aldermen in solemn state
At the Town Hall in council sate ;
They hear their mayor his foul wrongs state.
The case is put ; it seemed quite clear
That the mayor's daughter (*Rosy* dear)
Could not through *Pepper Gate* have run
Had not the bars been left undone.
They pass a law to close the gate
Through which the wild *Rose* sought her mate.

The townsmen smile : say they, ' What for,
When steed is gone, close stable door ?
When stolen the daughter, all too late
It is to close the *Pepper Gate*.'

The fruit-gardens outside the walls at Chester are called the Kailyards.

An old Welsh lullaby seems to allude to some such match as that described in the preceding verses.

Gurru, Gurru, Gurru i' Gaer,
I briodi merch y Maer.

i.e. Trotting, trotting, trotting to Chester
To marry the Mayor's daughter.

Playing at ball was a common sport for grown-up ladies in auld lang syne. In the ballad of ' The Brave Earl Brand ' is the following :

Now where is the lady of this hall ?
She's out with her maids a playing at the ball.

Again, the ballad of ' Barbara Livingston ' begins thus :

Four-and-twenty ladies fair
Were playing at the ba',
And out came Margaret Livingston
The flower amang them a'.

Another old ballad, ' The Cruel Brother,' or the ' Bride's Testament,' begins thus :

There were three ladies played at the ba'
With a heigho and a lily gay.
There came a knight and played o'er them a',
As the primrose spreads so sweetly.

Easter Song.

Sung by the children in the Wirral when they come round ' *Pace Egging.*'

PLEASE, Mr. *Whiteley*,
    Please give us an *Easter* egg.
    If you do not give us one
    Your hen shall lay an addled one,
    Your cock shall lay a stone.

Old *Mab*'s Curse.

Tradition of the Mynshull family.

'Sir,—There is a tradition in our family which has never been printed. I therefore send you a copy. I am a descendant of the 'pius' lady whose threat has been *so* prophetic, that, although allied to many of the best Cheshire and Lancashire families, and many broad acres once claimed us as their masters, not a single yard or *brick* can we now boast in either county.

'JOHN B. MINSHULL.'

MABEL's dole of pius fame,
From royal blude they say she kame.
Poor and needee foulkes doe telle
The *Mynshulles* land no one dare selle ;
For 'old *Mab*'s curse' on hym wold lighte
That e'er should selle lande, stone, or bighte :
His house shall come to povertee.
Until another *Mab* wee see,
Centries rounde thys globe shalle rolle
Upon its axis on the pole,
Ere *Mynshulles* house againe shall thryve,
For selling '*Mab*'s' lande, huts, and style.
Such penance shalle his sons longe suffer,
And thanke the Virgin 'tis no rouffer.
Blest be the son of all its race
Who thus *Mab*'s dole shall replace.

William de Mynshulle, somewhere about the time of Edward I., married *Mabella*, daughter of Thomas de Erdeswick. This is the only 'Mab' I find in the pedigree of the family.—ED.

DRIVING THE DEER IN LYME PARK.

The Loves of Sir *Robert Barton* and *Margery Legh*.

A Tale of Lyme.

PART I.

I.

FLOATED a lay on the evening air,
    A lay of the blithest melodie,
And never reclined a form more fair
    Than sang thus under the greenwood tree.

II.

'Oh, I love to roam o'er the bright green lea,
Where the birds carol wildly, and all is free—
To follow the course of the murmuring brooks
Through their quiet glens and their shady nooks.

III.

'I love to track the purple moor,
    And gather the heather bells,
And seek within for the tiny forms
    That sport in their fairy cells.

IV.

'I love to gaze on the sunlit spray
    That plays o'er lichened rocks,
And the hue of every gem and flower
    In varied beauty mocks.

V.

'The forest glades have charms for me :
    I love in their shady bowers
To while away the livelong day,
    And dream through the fleeting hours.

VI.

'And I will roam through the woodland green,
    Or on mossgrown bank recline.
There's never knight in this land, I ween,
    Hath claims on this heart of mine.

VII.

'I'll ever be a gladsome maid,
    And list to no lover's tongue ;
There's never knight in this countrie
    Shall hold me a captive long.'—

VIII.

'Right bravely said !' Thus a knight's voice rang
    Quite close to the maiden's ear ;
'But, an thou do this, no priest will shrive
    Thee of broken hearts, I fear.'—

IX.

' I shall be ladye of many lands,'
    Quoth she, ' that shall be mine own.'—
' But what will thy broadlands do for thee
    When thou shalt be sad and lone ?

X.

'O fleetly may pass the summer hour,
    And short is pleasure's day ;
But when winter comes, the wintry frost
    Will turn those dark locks gray.'—

XI.

' Now, call you gallantry this, sir knight,
    A maid thus to annoy ?
To speak to her of the lonesome night
    Whilst all her days are joy ?

XII.

' And dost call thyself a gallant knight
    To tell me this at *Lyme* ?
To frighten me with cold winter's blight
    All in my summer's prime ?'—

XIII.

' Not always in summer's dress divine,
    A maiden blithe and free,
Thou wilt on the soft sward thus recline
    Under the greenwood tree.'—

XIV.

'Oh troth, art thou not a doleful knight,
   And croakest ruefullie?
And thinkest thou thus to win the heart
   Of blithesome *Margaret Legh*?'

XV.

Then up she sprang, and she left her lute
   Under the greenwood tree;
Alone with quick step she sought the hall;
   The knight sighed pensivelie.

PART II.

I.

Hark! hark! what mean those yells and shouts—
   Those footsteps clattering near?
On, on with whirlwind rush they come,
   The bounding wild red deer.

II.

A moment's pause, then in they plunge
   Deep midst the watery surge,
And lave their flanks in th' ice-cold flood,
   Reluctant to emerge;

III.

But spurred on by pursuers' cries,
   Dash up the sedgy shore,
Shake from their sides the dripping spray,
   Then rush on as before.

IV.

Now fiercer grown, they madly bound
  O'er hill, through brake, o'er plain ;
Behind they leave the distanced throng,
  The deepest shades to gain.

V.

Their flashing blood-shot eyes now tell
  How mad has grown their wrath;
The boldest wight in all that crowd
  Would fear to cross their path.

PART III.

I.

A maiden and a knight reclined
  Under the greenwood tree,
When a rushing sound is heard behind
  Advancing rapidly.

II.

On sprang the deer with rapid bound,
  Their wild eyes flashing fire;
A stag of ten his antlers lowered
  To vent on them his ire.

III.

Upsprang at once that stalwart knight
  To save the fainting fair ;
The beast rushed on in fury's might,
  Like tiger from his lair.

IV.

The death-sick maiden swooned away ;
  The knight his falchion dyed
In the heart's blood of maddened foe,
  As the antler pierced his side !

V.

See from the torn and gaping wound
  Life's blood is welling fast ;
And deadly pale the brave knight turned,
  And sank to earth at last.

VI.

Slowly the maiden oped her eyes,
  And gently raised her head ;
The knight lay stretched out by her side,
  Close by the red deer dead.

VII.

The trickling blood she tried to staunch,
  That gushed fast from his side ;
'How have I scorned thy faithful love !
  To save *me, thou* hast died !'

VIII.

Too late retainers hurry round ;
  With grief the sight they see ;
The knight they bear unto the hall,
  And soon the leech came he.

PART IV.

I.

Long, long, Sir *Robert Barton* lay
  His life in jeapordie,
And ever by his side was seen
  The weeping *Margaret Legh.*

II.

And when at length his sense returned,
  The glance that met his own
Soon spoke of what the maiden felt,
  The love she durst not own.

III.

That glance restored his fleeting life,
  And when his suit he pressed,
The maid looked down, and sobbing hid
  Her blushes on his breast.

IV.

' Well wot I that thou lovest me well,
  And wouldest for me have died ;
Oh take me to thy noble heart—
  Thy loving willing bride.'

V.

More brightly green now seemed the woods,
  More brightly green the lea ;
The leaves shone brighter in the sun,
  All on the greenwood tree.

VI.

The heather bell more purple hung
On the fresh breezy moor ;
The lavrock carolled forth his song
More blithely than before.

VII.

With rainbow colours shone the dew,
Kissed by the warm sunshine ;
The lichened rocks shewed softer hue,
Sweeter the eglantine.

VIII.

But sweeter than the eglantine,
Or rose that dewdrop sips,
Was *Margery*'s breath, Sir *Robert* vowed,
Oft as he pressed her lips.

IX.

Her beaming eyes were lovelier far
Than blue of cloudless sky ;
Her gladsome voice more charmed his ear
Than lavrock soaring high.

X.

The scented sigh of th' evening breeze
Stole through the greenwood tree,
And seemed in murmurs soft to bless
The knight and *Margery*.

Margery (daughter of Sir Peter Legh of Lyme and Haydock, knighted by Henry VIII.) married Sir Robert Barton of Smithill's Hall, near Bolton, to whose family it came by the marriage of Joan, sole heiress of Sir Rafe Radcliffe, with Robert Barton Esq. of Holme.

The ancient custom of driving the red deer through the water at Lyme has for several years been in abeyance.

Wilson, the historian, gives a curious account of his providential escape whilst stag-hunting, when a youth and follower of the Earl of Essex, as follows :—

'Sir Peter Legh of Lyme, in Cheshire, invited my lord to hunt the stagg ; and having a great stagg in chase and many gentlemen in pursuit, the stagg took soyle, and divers (whereof I was one) alighted, and stood with our swords drawne, to have a cut at him at his coming out of the water. The staggs there being wonderfully fierce and dangerous, made us youths more eager to be at him. But he escaped us all. And it was my misfortune to be hindered of my coming neare him, the waye being slipperie, by a falle : which gave occasion to some one who did not knowe mee to speake as if I had fallen through feare, which being told mee I left the stagg and followed the gentleman who first spoke it. But I founde him of that cold temper that it seemed his words made an escape from him, as by his denial and repentance it appeared. But this made mee more violent in the pursuit of the stagg, to recover my reputation. And I happened to be the onlie horseman in, when the dogs sett him up at bay, and approaching neare him on horsebacke he broke through the dogs and ran at mee, and tore my horse's side with his hornes close by my thighe. Then I quitted my horse, and grewe more cunning (for the doggs had set him up againe); stealing behind him with my sworde and cut his hamstrings, and then got upon his backe and cut his throate, which as I was doing the companie came up and blamed my rashness for running such a hazard.'

The Old Brown Forest.

I.

BROWN forest of *Mara* ! whose bounds were of yore
From *Kellsborrows* castle outstretched to the shore,
Our fields and our hamlets afforested then
That thy beasts might have covert, unhoused were
    our men.

II.

Our king the first *William*, *Hugh Lupus* our earl,
Then poaching I ween was no sport for a churl :
A noose for his neck who a snare should contrive,
Who skinned a dead buck was himself flayed alive.

III.

Our *Normandy* nobles right dearly I trow
They loved in the forest to bend the yew bow;
They wound their 'recheat' and their 'mort' on the horn,
And they laughed the rude chase of the *Saxon* to scorn.

IV.

In right of his bugles and greyhounds to seize
Waif, pannage, ajistment, and wind-fallen trees,
His knaves through our forest *Ralph Kingsley* dispersed,
Bow-bearer in chief to Earl *Randle* the first.

V.

This horn the grand forester wore at his side
Whene'er his liege lord chose a hunting to ride :
By Sir *Ralph* and his heirs for a century blown,
It passed from their lips to the mouth of a *Done.*

VI.

Oh then the proud falcon, unloosed from the glove,
Like her master below played the tyrant above ;
While faintly, more faintly, were heard in the sky
The silver-toned bells as she darted on high.

VII.

Then, roused from sweet slumber, the ladie highborn
Her palfrey would mount at the sound of the horn ;
Her palfrey uptossed his rich trappings in air
And neighed with delight such a burden to bear.

VIII.

Versed in all woodcraft and proud of her skill,
Her charms in the forest were lovelier still ;
The abbot rode forth from the abbey so fair,
Nor loved the sport less when a bright eye was there.

IX.

Thou *Palatine* prophet ! whose fame I revere
(Woe be to that bard who speaks ill of a seer),
Forewarned of thy fate, as our legends report
Thou wert born in a forest and 'clemmed' in a court.

X.

Now goading thine oxen, now urging amain
Fierce monarchs to battle on *Bosworth*'s red plain ;
' A foot with two heels and a hand with three thumbs '—
Good luck to the land when this prodigy comes !

XI.

' Steeds shall by hundreds seek masters in vain
Till under their bellies their girths rot in twain ! '
'Twill need little skill to interpret this dream
When o'er the Brown Forest we travel by steam.

XII.

Here hunted the *Scot* whom, too wise to shew fight,
No war save the war of the woods could excite :
His learning they say did his valour surpass,
Though a hero when armed with a couteau de chasse.

XIII.

Ah then came the days when to *England*'s disgrace
A king was her quarry and warfare her chase :
Old *Noll* for their huntsman ! a Puritan pack !
With psalms on their tongues but with blood on their track.

XIV.

Then *Charlie* our king was restored to his own,
And again the blithe horn in the forest was blown ;
Steeds from the desert then crossed the blue wave
To contend on our turf for the prizes he gave,

XV.

Ere *Bluecap* and *Wanton* taught foxhounds to scurry
With music in plenty.   Oh where was the hurry ?
When each nag wore a crupper, each squire a pigtail,
When our toast, ' the Brown Forest !' was drunk in brown ale.

XVI.

The fast ones come next with a wild fox in view,
' Ware hole !' was a caution then heeded by few;
Opposed by no cops, by no fences confined,
O'er winbush and heather they swept like the wind.

XVII.

Behold in the soil of our forest once more
The sapling takes root as in ages of yore,
The oak of old *England* with branches outspread,
The pine tree above them uprearing his head.

XVIII.

Where twixt the whalebones the widow sat down
Who forsook the Black Forest to dwell in the Brown ;
There, where the flock on sweet herbage once fed,
The blackcock takes wing, and the fox-cub is bred.

XIX.

This timber the storms of the ocean shall weather,
And sail o'er the waves as we sailed o'er the heather ;
Each plant of the forest, when launched from the stocks,
May it run down a foeman as we do a fox.

Stanza 4. The master forestership of the whole was conferred by Randle I., in the twelfth century, on Ralph de Kingsley, to hold the same by the tenure of a horn. Amongst other perquisites claimed by the master forester were the following: 'And claymeth to have the latter pannage in the said forest, and claymeth to have windfallen wood; he claymeth to have all money for agistment of hogs within the said forest . . . . and as to wayfe, he claymeth to have every wayfe and stray beast as his own, after proclamation shall be made, and not challenged as the manner is.'—*Ormerod*, vol. ii. p. 52.

Stanza 5. 'When'er his liege lord chose a hunting to ride,' &c. Cheshire tradition asserts that the ancient foresters were bound to use this horn, and attend in their office with two white greyhounds, whenever the earl was disposed to honour the Forest of Delamere with his presence in the chase.—*Ormerod*, vol. ii. p. 33.

Stanza 5. 'It passed from their lips to the mouth of a Done.' The Dones of Utkuylon succeeded the Kingsleys, or chief foresters. On the termination of this line in 1715, the forestership passed to Richard Ardune, and through him to the Lords Alvanley.

Stanzas 9, 10, 11. Refer to Robert Nixon and his prophecies.

Stanza 12. 'Here hunted the Scot,' &c. King James I.

Stanza 15. 'Ere Bluecap and Wanton,' &c. Two Cheshire hounds.—Vide vol. i. p. 212, *Daniel's Rural Sports*.

Stanza 17. 'Behold on the soil of our forest once more,' &c. By the Act of Parliament passed in 1812 for the enclosure of Delamere Forest, one moiety of the whole is appropriated as a nursery for timber.

Stanza 18. 'Where twixt the whalebones the widow sat down.' Maria Holingsworth, a German, the widow of an English soldier. She built herself a hut near two ribs of a whale in Delamere Forest, where she lived many years. For an account of her curious life, vide 'Notes of a Lady of Quality.'

The district extending from the banks of the Mersey to the south boundary of the late forest was designated as the Forest of Mara, whilst that of Mondrem stretched in the direction of Nantwich.

The Mayor of *Chester*'s Speech to *James I.* on his Return out of *Scotland*, A.D. 1617.

GREAT kinge, to bidd thee welcome behold I
Doe speake, although my mouthe stand by ;
I'le doe my best, but hee can doe much better ;
Hee is book-learned, I ne'er knew a letter.
When yesterday the post did tideings bringe
That I sholde see you here (our royall kinge),
For my part into an ague I did falle,
And greatelie gloppened were my brethren all,
But least your Matie shold think us slacke,
Each one of us did take a pinte of sacke,
Armour of proof, the best thinge wee colde find
To cheare our heartes and ease a trobled mind.
We went about to muster upp our forces,
To meet you at *Botone* ; but we wanted horses.
Our foote cloathes also by ratts and mice offended,
In soe short space cold not be patched and mended.
Therefore this stage that holdes us here at large
Was wisely founded at the cittyes chardge.
These men in scarlett whom you plainlie see
Have been in this place of Matie,
The other in purple gownes that doe appeare
Are like to weare my stuffe another yeare.

The streets as you doe pass on either hand
Are sweetlie flored wth gravell and wth sand ;
The conduit at ye Crosse if you marke well,
Is newlie painted, you may know by th' smell.
The place against it is the place where I
Doe sit in all my pompe and dignitie,
While I doe justice, be itt right or wronge,
To the rich or poore, or old or younge.
St. *Peter*'s Church, where I am often seene,
Stands neare unto itt, it's but a leape betweene ;
Where ev'ry Sunday to my poore power,
Sleeping and waking, I do stand an hower.
Your grace may see our horses have had spungeing,
And eke your wine shal be without blundring ;
Butt in this one thinge pray by me be rul'd,
Doe not drinke of itt untill it be mul'd,
But if you see itt looke blue on either side,
Then supp it up, you need no other guide.
Our citty is not rich, yett *God* be thanked
Wth no small chardge we have p'cured a banquett,
Fowre pound it cost, besides I am afraid
The carriage of it down is yett unpaid.
If you had come to dinner, wthout boast
You shold have eate wth mee both sodd and roast.
For though I saie itt, I could have let you loose
Into ye flanke of a fatt stubble goose.
A cupp with gold unto your grace I'le bringe,
In hope to us you'le give a better thinge,
For I'le be sworne itt did goe neare our heart
When from so manie gold angells wee did parte.

But much good doe it you we'le neare repent,

Since they are gone, they might have been worse spent.

Some say of mee you meane to make a knight,

Rather take a haltar and hang mee outright,

That it may nere be said it came to passe

That you bestowed it upon *Balaam*'s asse :

Therefore I humblie crave I may goe free,

And give itt to the Maior of *Coventree*.

Thus from my speech abruptlie I will breake,

If yowle knowe more, heare the Recorder speake.

Line 2. 'Mouthe' means Recorder.

Line 14. 'Botone.' Boughton, a suburb of Chester.

Line 19. 'These men in scarlett,' &c. Aldermen who have been mayors.

Line 21. 'The other in purple gownes,' &c. Aldermen who have never been mayors.

Line 23. 'The streets as you doe passe,' &c. In the churchwarden's accounts of the Holy Trinity parish at Chester, A.D. 1617, is the following item : ' For rushes and sand, 23rd August, to straw the street before the church against our precious Soveraine Lord King James, his comming to the citty with manie of his nobles the same daye in th' afternoone. Holmes Man, No. 2177, Harl. Bibl.' In an old ballad (Childe Vyet) we find mention made of strewing the streets with gravel on grand occasions.

> Tween Mary Kirk and that castle
> Was all spread o'er with garl,
> To keep the lady and her maidens
> From tramping on the marl.

Line 46. 'Sodd.' Sodden, i.e. boiled.

Line 55. 'Some say of mee you meane to make a knight,' &c. Charles Fytton (by others called Mutton) was Mayor at the time of the royal visit in 1617, and refused an offered knighthood. On Tuesday, August 21, 1617, King James I. came to Chester. The Mayor and Aldermen took their places on a scaffold, railed and hung about with green, and there in a most grave and seemly manner they awaited the arrival of his Majestie. At which time, after a learned speech delivered by the Recorder, the Mayor presented to the King a fair standing cup with a cover double gilt, and therein an hundred Jacobusses in gold. The King attended a sumptuous banquet, prepared at the city cost, which, being ended, the King departed to Vale Royal. At his departure the order of knighthood was offered to Mr. Edward Mutton, the Mayor, but he refused the same. The name, it appears, was Button, not Mutton. Hopkinson has preserved in his manuscripts the above satirical account of this visit in verse. 'After the banquet (according to Webb) the King made the house of Vale Royal his royal court, where he solaced himself for four days, and took pleasing entertainment in his disports in the Forest.'

Cheshire Recipes for Hooping-Cough.

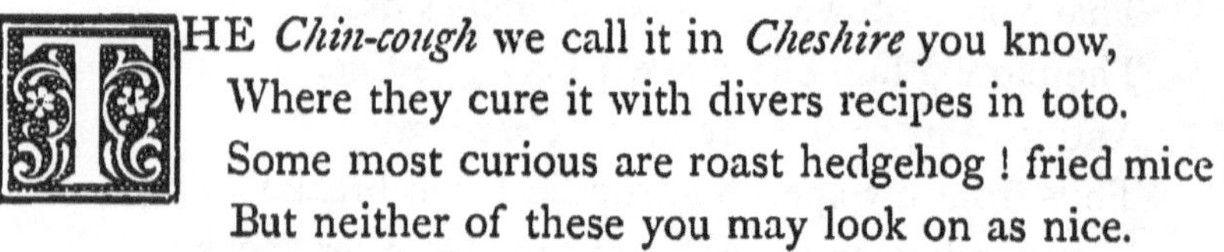

HE *Chin-cough* we call it in *Cheshire* you know,
Where they cure it with divers recipes in toto.
Some most curious are roast hedgehog ! fried mice !
But neither of these you may look on as nice.
Then some hold a live frog quite close to their lips,
'Tis said the frog thus from them hooping-cough sips.
An old crone grumbled once, ' Her lad's cough would not go,
Though he'd sucked two toads to death.' She really said so.
Here's another recipe—you must find out a dame
Who, though she has married, has not changed her name.
At once you must ask bread and butter from her :
This, they say, of *all* cures is *the* sovereign cure.

' Perhaps no diseases, except epilepsy and the ague, have more curious, local, and peculiar cures than exist for hooping-cough. A preventive for it in Ireland is to pass the child three times under the belly of an ass, muttering a prayer at the same time addressed to our Saviour and his mother. In Gloucestershire a small quantity of hair taken from the nape of the child's neck, then rolled up in meat and given to a dog, transfers the disease to him. In Hampshire the sufferer is recommended to drink new milk out of a cup made from the variegated holly. In Shropshire the child must drink only out of an ivy-wood cup. In Warwickshire they calcine and use the " Devil's Thumb " (or Gryphæa incurva). In Yorkshire owl broth is recommended. In Norfolk a house spider is caught and put in a muslin bag, and pinned over the mantelpiece. Whilst the spider lives the cough remains. The spider's death and patient's cure are simultaneous. Hairs plucked from the cross on a donkey's back, and worn in a black silk bag round the neck of the suffering child, is considered a specific. In Devonshire you are carried fasting into three parishes. In Cornwall a slice of bread and butter or cake belonging to a married couple whose names are John and Joan is supposed to supersede all drugs. You may also at your option, if a sufferer from whooping-cough, drink the remainder of the milk left by a tame fox, or be dragged backwards through a bramble bush, or pass the afflicted child under a bramble rooted on both sides, or let it be breathed on by a piebald horse, or give it hol water out of a silver chalice, which is not to be touched.'—Notes and Queries.

Cheshire Cheese.

I.

CHESHIRE man set sail for *Spain*,
  To deal in merchandise,
And when he arrived there
  A *Spaniard* he espies,

II.

Who says, 'You saucy *Englishman*,
  Rich fruits and spices fine
Our land produces twice a year,
  There's no such like in thine.'

III.

The *Englishman* he stepped aside,
  And took a *Cheshire* cheese,
And says, 'You saucy *Spaniard* dog,
  You've no such fruit as these.

IV.

'Your land produces twice a year,
  Rich fruits and spice you say,
But what I in my hands do hold
  Our land gives twice a day.

Cheshire Cheese.

Another Version.

I.

CHESHIRE man went o'er to *Spain*,
  To trade and merchandise,
And when arrived across the main
  A *Spaniard* there he spies.

II.

'Thou *Cheshire* man,' quoth he, 'look here,
  These fruits and spices fine
Our country yields these twice a year ;
  Thou hast not such in thine.'

III.

The *Cheshire* man soon sought the hold,
  Thence brought a *Cheshire* cheese,
'You *Spanish* dog, look here,' saith he,
  'You have not such as these.

IV.

'Your land produces twice a year
  Spices and fruits you say,
But such as in my hand I bear
  Our land yields twice a day.'

In singing the song each line is repeated.

A Che - shire man sail'd in - to Spain, To
trade for mer - chan - dise; When he ar - riv - ed
from the main, A Span - iard him e - spies, . . . a
Span - iard him e - spies.

PIANO.
Who said, you Eng - lish rogue, look here, What
fruits and spi - ces fine Our land pro-du - ces
twice a year; Thou hast not such in thine ... thou

hast not such in thine.

The Story of *Horseley* Hall.

[Horseley Hall, once the seat of the Powells, a family now extinct, stands on the borders of Denbighshire and Cheshire. The Powells were the possessors of the Abbey lands at Birkenhead. The Sir Thomas mentioned in the following tale died A.D. 1694. The following appeared in 'Sharpe's London Magazine,' vol. i. p. 289. There is unluckily no clue to the author. I have to thank Mr. Brushfield's kindness and research for enabling me to add the story of Horseley Hall to my collection.—E.]

I

HE Lady was sitting alone in her grief,
   Yet her proud flashing eye scorned to weep for relief,
   Whilst these half muttered words from her pale lips comprest
   Gave vent to the passion that swelled in her breast :

II.

'Am I thus then cast off—like a plaything laid by ?
Are his vows all forgot ! hath he wearied his eye ?
Hath his fickle heart (yearning again to be free)
Learnt another is younger and fairer than me ?

III.

' Where's the love he once swore should be strong in all time,
Should soften our age as it gladdened our prime ?
The flame then so hot is grown suddenly cold,
Like a dream that is fled, like a tale that was told.

IV.

' His want of affection and love I could bear
With a heart ill at ease, and a proud careless air ;
But to meet such a slight, such a mark of disdain,
Oh my *God* ! it o'erpowers and maddens my brain.

V.

' Was his easy neglect not enough of disgrace
That he needs must caress here my maid to my face ?
'Twere better to die, than a byeword to live :
Life to me now no pleasure, save vengeance, can give.'

VI.

'Twas a sight full of dread, in that old chamber dark,
The passion that worked midst such beauty to mark ;
Far better to meet with a she-wolf at bay
Than encounter a woman when baulked in her way.

VII.

She heard a low knock, and serene grew her face
Like the sea when a cloud passeth o'er without trace;
As, the door softly opening, her maiden stept in,
You'd have thought her a creature too lovely for sin.

VIII.

Said the Lady, with voice which dissembled her hate,
' I forgot that the evening was drawing on, *Kate* :
Thou shalt tire me, good wench, to the best of thy power,
For Sir *Thomas* I hope will be here in an hour.'

IX.

Her forehead is bound with a chaplet of pearl,
And her dark raven locks o'er her snowy neck curl ;
Oh never I ween had that lady so fair
Seemed fairer than then, or more sprightly her air.

X.

She leaned through the casement her beautiful head:
' He is coming at last ! He is coming ! ' she said.
' Now nearer and nearer his horse's hoofs fall;
He will quickly be here : let us haste to the hall.'

XI.

Through the gallery long the unfortunate pair
Arrived at the head of the carved oaken stair,
When the maid, by her mistress (as old people tell)
On a sudden pushed down, o'er the banister fell.

XII.

One instant her white robes all fluttered in air,
The next she was dashed at the foot of the stair ;
You may still see the stain on the mould'ring wood
Where the floor of the hall was bespattered with blood.

XIII.

As the Lady descended the staircase alone
She thought she once heard her in agony moan ;
But when on the last step she listened, no sound
Save the clock's solemn tick broke the silence around.

XIV.

When Sir *Thomas* and she o'er the dead body met,
There was that in her eye man might never forget;
One glance spoke the whole of her heart's deadly hate,
And told how the maiden had come by her fate.

XV.

Neither uttered a word—but their souls felt within
That each knew the whole of the other one's sin.
As they gazed on the blood-dabbled face of the dead,
They felt that in life all their pleasure was fled.

XVI.

'Twas deemed that *Kate*'s foot slipped, for none saw the blow :
Yet at times there were whisperings, though secret and low,
That some terrible sight did their Lady appal
Whenever she ventured to pass through that hall.

XVII.

They buried the corpse in the pleasant churchyard
At the foot of a yew by the western gate hard,
And still doth a tomb with a quaint arch built high
Mark the place where the bones of that young creature lie.

XVIII.

Yet a curse seemed to brood o'er the house : the proud dame
Soon to foreign lands passed, nor back ever she came.
In a convent she sought, by prayer, fasting, and tears,
To atone for that deed all the rest of her years.

XIX.

When Sir *Thomas* died early, the last of his race,
No kinsman attended his bones to their place;
But buried by strangers, uncared for, unwept,
With his fathers in *Birkenhead* Abbey he slept.

Bradshaw the Regicide.

In Stockport church is the following entry of the birth of Bradshaw the regicide:

'A.D. 1602. John, the sonne of Henry Bradshaw of Marple, was baptized the 10th of December.'

It is said he wrote the following lines on a stone in Macclesfield churchyard:

M Y brother *Henry* must heir the land,
My brother *Frank* must be at his command:
Whilst I, poor *Jack*, will do that
That all the world shall wonder at.

The Nutwoman.

A Legend of Knutsford.

I.

 WOMAN lived at *Knutsford* once,
  The town where King *Canute*
  Once wet his royal foot
Some say, but some call this a bounce.

II.

Her living this old woman gained
  By the sale of her nuts,
  For which youngsters drew cuts :
On her the town halfpence all rained.

III.

She died—and 'twas found in her will
  She *would* rest her old head
  On a sack (when quite dead)
Which boys with the best nuts should fill.

IV.

Neighbours laughed ; but—but me no buts—
  When they buried the dame
  She'd a pillow the same
She had willed—a bag full of nuts !

THE OLD NUTWOMAN.

V.

She had not in her grave lain long
  When these nuces she found
  A nuisance underground
She ne'er thought to nuts would belong.

VI.

All sides were bumpy she might choose ;
  She could no way get ease :
  The nuts proved worse than peas
That *Pilgrim* once put in his shoes.

VII.

Desp'rate at length, one starry night
  An upwards spring she gave ;
  And jumped out of her grave,
And dragged her nuts up to the light.

VIII.

She sat herself on tombstone then,
  And cracked every nut
  With her teeth or her foot,
Then slipped to her coffin again.

IX.

And smooth she folded up her sack,
  But first she shook it out,
  To get all nuts without ;
As a pillow then put it back.

X.

She ev'ry nut had cracked one save,
 Which when she shook the sack
 Bounding out then, good lack,
Fell into a hole near her grave.

XI.

So ends the tale of th' old nut crone.
 The story must be true,
 For high a nut-tree grew,
And there it still grows—if—not—gone.

1st Stanza. 'The town where King Canute,' &c. One of the derivations of Knutsford is Canute's Ford.

Belfry Rhymes.

Wybunbury Church.

IF for to ring you do come here,
  You must ring well with hand and ear ;
  And if you ring in spur or hat,
  A quart of ale you pay for that ;
And if a bell you overthrow,
Sixpence you pay before you go.
These laws are old, they are not new,
Therefore the clerk must have his due.

Middlewych.

*IDDLEWYCH* is a pretty town,
Seated in a valley,
With a church and market cross,
And eke a bowling alley.
All the men are loyal there ;
Pretty girls are plenty ;
Church and King, and down with the Rump,
There's not such a town in twenty.

The stones of the Market Cross were removed in 1809. Middlewych cannot now be called a pretty town, but, as Archdeacon Wood remarks, 'Before the canal interfered with its brook, and when the black and white houses (now fast disappearing), with their quaint devices and varied patterns, filled the valley and clustered round the old church, it might then have deserved the epithet given it in these lines.'—The Cavalier toast marks the date.

Epitaph in Middlewych *Churchyard, near the Priest's Door.*

Here lies *Anne,* wife of *Daniel Barker,* who died *July* 3rd, 1778, Aged 77.

Some have children, some have none,
But here lies the mother of twenty-one.

James Price.

[James Price was hung in chains on Trafford Green in 1790, for robbing the Warrington Mail, and remained there till 1820, when the pole was taken down, the place having been enclosed. In his skull was found a robin's nest.]

OH ! *James Price* deserved his fate :
Naught but *Robbing* in his pate
Whilst alive, and now he's dead
Has still *Robin* in his head.
High he swings for *Robbing* the *Mail*,
But his brain of *Robin female*
Still is quite full ; though out of breath,
The passion e'en survives his death.

Blessing the Brine.

[On Ascension day, in days long past, the inhabitants of Nantwych (or Hellath Wen, as the town used to be called) used to assemble in gala dress round the 'Old Biat' salt pit, which was ornamented for the occasion with flowers and all procurable rustic finery, and pass the day in dancing, feasting, and merriment. This was called Blessing the Brine.]

I.

CHORUS.

WREATHS of varied hues we bring,
Flowers of the early spring,
Hand in hand we join a ring,
Round Old *Biat* pit to sing,
God bless the Brine.

II.

Gather 'Paigles,' bring '*Lent* Lilies,'
Of 'Sweet *Nancy*' tie up posies ;
Add 'Ladies smock' all silver white,
'Marsh Marygolds,' childhood's delight.
Chorus, Wreaths &c.

III.

Bawme the Old Pit with ribbands gay,
Torn from the groves green boughs display,
Whilst we in holiday attire
Lead the fleet dance both child and sire.
Chorus, Wreaths &c.

IV.

Sound the lound trimbrel, beat the drum,
Nor let the clarion's throat be dumb,
Here let us feast, and sing, and play ;
Ascension's feast's our holiday.
        Chorus, Wreaths &c.

V.

Long since, before the *Roman* host
In pomp of war old *Cheshire* crost,
This pit our fathers' labouring saw,
The garnered hoards from earth to draw.
        Chorus, Wreaths &c.

VI.

We bless the author of all good,
For that which savours all our food ;
Of gifts on man that showered are,
What gift to this can we compare?
        Chorus, Wreaths &c.

VII.

The finny treasures of the deep,
The flocks that climb the mountain steep,
All food spread over plain and lea,
Without our salt would tasteless be?
        Chorus, Wreaths &c.

VIII.

Pledge of true friendship, for its sake
Wild *Arabs* scorn their faith to break ;

Nor will their truth e'er prove at fault
'Towards him with whom they've eaten salt.
Chorus, Wreaths &c.

IX.

We envy not climes where we're told
The rivers run o'er sands of gold,
Nor sigh we for *Golconda's* mine
Whilst we can boast our pits of brine.
Chorus, Wreaths &c.

X.

We hear in foreign lands, salt sick,
The wild herds roam in search of lick.
Who by words may dare to measure
The price of this heavenly treasure.
Chorus, Wreaths &c.

XI.

So when *Ascension*'s morn appears,
As years succeeding follow years,
Shall ' Hellath Wen ' her children see
United here for mirth and glee.
Chorus, Wreaths &c.

XII.

And as our *Saviour* on this day
Triumphant rose from earth away,
So shall our thanks to Heaven arise,
So let our praises reach the skies.

XIII.

CHORUS.

Wreaths of varied hue we bring,
Flowers of the early spring,
Hand in hand we form a ring,
Round Old *Biat* pit to sing,
God bless the Brine.

No. 2 Stanza. *Paigle*, Cheshire for a Primrose or Cowslip. *Lent Lilies*, Daffodils. *Sweet Nancy*, Narcissus. *Lady's Smock*, the Cuckoo flower.

No. 3. To bawme is to adorn, to dress up.

No. 6. Salt was supposed never to be used at a witch festival. Homer speaks of θειος ἁλσ. Salt used in England to be considered as proof against all demoniac influence, and was and is given in some parts of England to a new-born babe, to preserve it from the devil until screened from him by baptism. The present (not uncommon in Cheshire and Lancashire', on its first visit, of an egg, a handful of salt, and a bunch of matches, is called "puddining."

No. 10. In America the deer and buffalo will traverse great distances, directed by instinct, at certain times of the year, to the Salt Lick.

The Old Man Outwitted.

[Supposed by Mr. Halliwell to date about the middle of the eighteenth century.]

I.

ET all lovers which around me do stand
    Be pleased to give ear to these lines I have penned,
    And when you have heard them I am sure you will
    It's a medicine to drive melancholy away.   [say,

II.

Its of an ancient farmer near *Chester* did dwell,
Whose name at the present I need not to tell :
He had an only daughter both charming and fair,
She quickly was drawn into *Cupid*'s snare.

III.

Her father indeed kept a servant man,
For to do his business, his name it was *John* ;
The maid was smitten with each glance of his eye,
That she never was easy out of his company.

IV.

They often together in private would walk
Alone in the garden, and pleasantly talk :
But pray give attention, and soon you shall hear
How this passion oft brought them into a snare.

V.

Her father one night to the window had got
Just over the place where these two lovers sat,
And heard ev'ry word that between them was said,
By which this unfortunate youth was betrayed.

VI.

' My dear,' said the young man, ' my love it is true,
And I have set my affections on you ;
I hope you'll remember the vows that are past,
And woe be to them who our comforts shall blast!'

VII.

The maiden immediately fell on her knee,
And said, ' If ever I prove the ruin of thee,
May all that I act in the world never thrive,
Nor I ever prosper while I am alive.'

VIII.

The old man retired then with a frown :
With a heart full inflamed he sat himself down,
Contriving some way for to part the young pair,
And how it was acted you quickly shall hear.

IX.

Next morning, right early, he called his man *John*,
And when that he into the parlour had come,
He said, ' I am bound to *London*, and that speedily ;
Speak up, are you willing to go along with me ?'

x.

'Dear honoured sir,' the young man replied,
'The thing you require shall not be denied ;
But in your journey I attentive shall be,
Because I am willing that city to see.'

xi.

Next morning for *London* they then did steer,
And soon did arrive at that city we hear :
Let innocent lovers be pleased to wait,
The truth of the subject I soon shall relate.

xii.

Next morning the old man arose,
And privately to a sea-captain he goes :
Saying, 'Sir, I am told you want lads for the sea,
And I have got a lad that will fit to a tee.'

xiii.

'Here's thirty bright guineas I'll freely give thee
If you can contrive to take him to the sea,
That he never more to old *England* may come.'
'A match,' said the captain, 'that same shall be done.'

xiv.

A pressgang immediately up to him went,
And having secured him, on board he was sent
In tears to lament on the said roaring main,
Never expecting more to see his love again.

XV.

That day after dinner it happened so
That the captain's lady on board she would go ;
Walking the deck, her fair face for to fan,
And casting her eyes down did see this young man

XVI.

Sit close in a corner, his eyes full of tears,
His face pale as ashes, and heart full of fears ;
Which sight filled the lady with such discontent
That away to the captain that minute she went.

XVII.

Saying, 'What youth is that, love ? prithee tell me,
Because that he sitteth so melancholy.'
The captain straight called him ; the young man he came
With tears in his face ; then he asked him his name.

XVIII.

He told him his name with many a tear,
Likewise the cause of his coming here ;
From the truth of his love his ruin did rise,
Which drew many tears from the young lady's eyes.

XIX.

She begged for his liberty straight on her knee,
The captain did with her petition agree ;
He likewise returned him ten guineas of gold,
And gave him his freedom, and further, behold :

XX.

Saying, ' Get you to *Smithfield* away in a trice,
And buy you a nag about five guineas price ;
Get home before your master, now luck's in your hands,
And marry his daughter to make him amends.'

XXI.

The young man returned then his compliment,
And taking his leave to *Smithfield* he went,
Where he bought him a steed, and home did repair :
Now the cream of the jest be pleased to hear.

XXII.

Coming to his jewel he told her in brief
The cause of his sorrow, trouble, and grief;
And when she had heard she quickly agreed,
And early next morning they married indeed.

XXIII.

When they were married the young man did say,
' Go you to my father's without more delay,
And I'll tarry here a fancy to try :'
And how it was acted you'll hear bye and bye.

XXIV.

The bride being gone, to her chamber he goes,
Pulls off his coat, and puts on her clothes,
And sits himself down by the fire to spin :
Just as he was acting the old man came in.

XXV.

He lights from his horse and secured the same,
And into the house he immediately came,
Saying, ' Now, handsome daughter, I have taken care
To break the intrigues betwixt you and your dear.

XXVI.

' I have seen him far away from the shore,
Where waves do foam and the wild billows roar ;
You may now see another as fast as you please,
But as for your old love I've sent him to the seas.'

XXVII.

The young man immediately fell to the ground,
Pretending as though he had been in a swoon ;
In a passion then smiting his hands on his side,
' What have you done ? cruel master !' he cried.

XXVIII.

' Master with a vengeance !' the old man replied.
' Yes, yes, you're my master,' the young man he cried ;
' Oh pray but be easy, and to you I'll tell
The saddest misfortune that e're did befel.

XXIX.

' When my mistress heard I to *London* must go,
She craved, nay begged and intreated me so,
To be dressed in my clothes for to go along you,
Because she had a mind that city to view.'

XXX.

'Adzooks,' said the old man, 'what have I done ?
I have ruined my daughter, oh where shall I run ?
The *Devil's* bewitched me for coveting gold,
The life of my innocent daughter I've sold.'

XXXI.

The old man ran raving away to the barn,
And snatching a halter under his arm,
To a beam near at hand he immediately ran ;
With a rope round his neck away he swang.

XXXII.

The young man immediately whipped out his knife,
And cut him down e're he'd finished his life ;
Said, ' Dear sir, have patience, and do not complain,
And I'll do what I can for to fetch her again.'

XXXIII.

The old man he stared like a fox in a snare,
Saying, ' Bring my darling, whom I love so dear ;
And that very minute you bring her to town,
That moment I will pay thee five hundred pound.'

XXXIV.

' Nay that is not all, for to finish the strife,
I'll freely agree for to make her your wife;
And if that I forty years longer remain,
I never, no never, will cross her again.'

XXXV.

The young man replyed, ' I'm not free to trust,
But if you will give me a writing first,
I'll bring her, though never such hazards I run.'
' A match,' said the old man; ' that same shall be done.'

XXXVI.

He gave him a bond : having taken the same,
Away to the bride with the writing he came,
And told her the story of what he had done ;
It made the whole family laugh at the fun.

XXXVII.

Next morning he drest himself in his best clothes,
With his charming bride like a beautiful rose;
A walk to her father's house straight did they take,
And happened to meet him just ent'ring the gate.

XXXVIII.

They fell on their knees, and his blessing did crave,
The which he presently unto them gave ;
Then kissing his daughter, he said to his son,
Saying, ' *John*, you have me funned as sure as a gun.'

XXXIX.

They up from their knees and told him the truth :
He said, ' As you're both in the bloom of your youth,
I give you my blessing, and for my policy
Two thousand pounds you shall have when I die.'

XL.

You lovers in *Britain*, whoever you be,
That read these few lines take counsel of me ;
Don't matter loves crosses, howe'er thick they fall,
For marriage shall soon make amends for all.

The White Hind.

A Legend of St. John's Church, Chester.

I.

ING *Ethelred*, that man of grace,
  Of righteousness, for love
Resolved to bring upon his race
  A blessing from above.

II.

Like *Solomon* he sought to raise
  A temple rich and rare,
Where priests should chaunt their hymn of praise :
  Such was his daily care.

III.

The year six hundred four score nine
  He lay upon his bed ;
A dream sent by the power divine
  Breathed round his sleeping head.

IV.

A voice like music seemed to say,
  ' Arise ! where thou, O king,
Shalt see a milk white hind at bay,
  Thy pious work begin !'

V.

He rose, and conning o'er his dream,
    Eastward from *Chester* past ;
When hunter's cheer and hound's bay seem
    To near his footsteps fast.

VI.

There frowns o'er sparkling *Dee* a rock,
    (Above the anchorite cell
Where *Harold* was in monkish frock,
    His woes with prayer to quell ;

VII.

When, fled from *Hastings'* broken field
    Before the *Norman* host,
He cast away the sword and shield,
    His crown and kingdom lost).

VIII.

Here *Ethelred* a white hind saw
    By hunters sorely prest ;
The tears adown her face that faa
    Showed how she was distrest.

IX.

But as the king gazed on the scene,
    And the white hind at bay,
Hounds, huntsmen, and white hind I ween
    Melted in air away.

X.

Here to St. *John* King *Ethelred*
A wondrous fane upreared,
Where prayers were offered for the dead,
And the Great *God* revered.

XI.

Still on St. *John*'s church tower red,
Though lashed by storm and wind,
Stands carved in stone King *Ethelred*,
And near him the *White Hind*.

Stanza 3. In the 'Holy Life and History of St. Werburghe' we find the following stanza, which alludes to the date and builder of St. John's church :—

The yere of grace syxe hundredth foure score and nyen,
As sheweth myne auctour a Bryton Giraldus,
Kynge Ethelred myndynge most the blysse of heven
Edyfyed a collage chyrche notable and famous.
In the subbarbes of Chester pleasaunt and beauteous,
In the honour of God and the baptyst Saynt John,
With helpe of bysshop Wulfryce and good exortacyon.

Stanza 6. 'Above the anchorite cell,' &c. Giraldus Cambrensis mentions, as the tradition of this place (and one which, of course, was subsequent to the legend of the White Hind and the foundation of St. John's church), that King Harold, having survived the wounds received at the battle of Hastings, spent the rest of his life as an anchorite, in a cell near St. John's church, Chester.

Stanza 11. 'Stands carved in stone,' &c. This almost worn-out carving is on the west face of the tower. In consequence of a visit of Mr. Parker, and at the instigation and by the offer of a large subscription by our modern King Ethelred, the Marquis of Westminster, this church is being now thoroughly restored.

Sir *Percy Legh.*

Or the Legend of the Knight's Lowe and the Lady's Grave.

[In the park of Lyme is a beautiful conical hill crowned by a diadem of fir trees, called 'The Knight's Lowe;' and in another part of the estate a field, through which flows the Bollin, has always been known by the name of 'The Lady's Grave.' A white lady is said to haunt the house of Lyme, and listeners think they hear, in the still hours of the night, a sound as of a distant peal of bells. Sir Piers Legh married Joan, heiress of Sir Gilbert de Haydock; he died in Paris of wounds received at Agincourt, and was brought home for interment. His grandfather, Sir Thomas Danyers, distinguished himself at the battle of Cressy, amongst the chivalry of Chester there engaged; for 'he relieved the banner of his Earl, and took prisoner the Chamberlain of France, Tankerville.']

PART I.

I.

ARK ! what means that sound,
   That low and murmuring swell,
That dies away and comes again
   As 'twere a distant funeral knell.

II.

Hark, again that wail
   Borne up the passing gale,
Breaking from the neighbouring height
The solemn silence of the night

III.

And see the red deer clust'ring round
  Half startled listen to the sound,
And peer into the vacant space
  As though some strange sight met their gaze.

IV.

And shadowy forms now seem to pass
  With slow and solemn pace,
Bearing aloft some lifeless form
  To its last resting place.

V.

And flitting o'er the moonlight scene
  A female form appears in sight,
All dressed in white and silver sheen
  With many a pearl and gem bedight.

VI.

And following in the mourners' track,
  She wrings her hands as one that's fey,
And so the vision passes on
  To vanish with the light of day.

VII.

And who is this they bear along ?
  And who may be this maid in white ?
And what the legend yet unsung,
  And who be they who fright the night ?

PART II.

VIII.

High sounds of mirth rang through the hall
And mingled shouts of revelrie,
For there had feasted great and small,
Men both of high and low degree.

IX.

And courteous knight and courtly dame
Surveyed the scene right merrilie,
For blithely sped the frolic game
Within the halls of *Piers de Legh.*

X.

The bull which roamed the forest wide
Had given his carcase to the feast,
An arrow pierced his milk-white hide
And stretched in death the lordly beast.

XI.

The red deer bounded o'er the hill
E'en at the earliest streak of day,
The sleuth-hound followed on his track
And brought the noble stag to bay.

XII.

The heron, by the sedgy pool
Watching intent its finny prey,
Was startled by the merlin's cry,
And fell to grace the feast that day.

XIII.

And many a white-plumed swan beside,
　And fruits from many a foreign clime,
And costly wines, and dainties rare,
　The feast swelled that was held at *Lyme.*

XIV.

And flagons passed along the board
　Filled to the brim with foaming ale,
And goblets flashed with ruby wine,
　And merrily sped the glad wassail.

XV.

And now paced up and down the hall
　Lords and knights of high degree,
And towering high above them all
　The stalwart form of *Percy Legh.*

XVI.

And on his arm a maiden hung
　More beauteous far than all beside,
Whose love-lit eye and blushing cheek
　Told that she was Sir *Percy*'s bride.

XVII.

And now its summons spoke the gong
　Booming through the spacious hall,
When quick arranged the happy throng
　To thread the mazes of the ball.

XVIII.

And many a whispered vow was made,
   And many a flashing glance was thrown,
And many a gallant heart was pierced,
   And many a maiden's peace was flown.

PART III.

XIX.

Now with horse and with hound the gallant array
Were out on the moor at the break of the day,
To rouse the wild bull or the stag from his lair,
And gather fresh laurels from many a fair.

XX.

Overcome by the chase, overpowered by the heat,
They sought the fierce boar in his forest retreat;
Yet the foremost of all in this wild venerie
Was still the bold form of Sir *Percy de Legh.*

XXI.

And the bright eyes that met him when back he returned
Were more to him far than all praises he earned,
Whilst the plaudits of all men of every degree
Sank deep in the heart of the sweet *Joan de Legh.*

XXII.

Thus still prest time onwards : each day as it came
Brought its increase of bliss to the beauteous dame,
Whilst Sir *Percy* to all was so kindly and free,
And none were so happy as fair *Joan de Legh.*

PART IV.

XXIII.

Hark! what means that clarion shrill
Echoing from the neighbouring hill?
Paled the face of that lovely bride,
She feared it might some ill betide.

XXIV.

In many a gaudy colour drest
A horseman foreward quickly prest :
' Hasten ye all from cottage and hall,
The King hath need of his lieges all.'

XXV.

' To horse ! To horse !' Sir *Percy* cried,
Yet tried to soothe his startled bride.
' My trusty sword ! Nay never fear :
My shield and corslet, helm and spear !

XXVI.

' Nay, *Joan*, thou art a true knight's bride,
    And knowest well thy sovereign's call
Must be obeyed whene'er 'tis heard :
    The call of honour summons all.

XXVII.

' Still, love, those fears, and dry those tears,
    No coward's blood thy sweet frame warms ;
Thou would'st not with a coward mate,
    Nor take a craven to thy arms.'

XXVIII.

Thus spoke, then prest her to his heart,
Then quickly tore himself apart,
At once to saddle tree he sprung,
And to his horse the loose rein flung.

PART V.

XXIX.

And now the spurred and eager steed
Darting sprang forth with lightning speed;
She gave one look of agonie,
And saw her last of *Piers de Legh.*

XXX.

But there was one who loved him more,
Whose heart those parting tidings tore;
Who'd loved *Piers* more than all beside,
Before he *Joan* had made his bride.

XXXI.

Unwooed, poor *Blanche* had loved Sir *Piers;*
This love had cost her bitter tears.
Ah, wo worth *Blanche* ! wo worth the day !
When *Percy* wed another may !

XXXII.

What maid might view that noble form
And not to such a warrior warm,
Unknown 'twas ever to the knight
That he to *Blanche* was breath and light.

XXXIII.

Hid in a thicket's darkest gloom
She gazed on *Percy*'s lessening plume,
Then fainting sank to earth at last,
Her life's joy crushed, her life's joy past.

PART VI.

XXXIV.

Hail to *England*'s gallant king,
  His banner proudly floats on high,
And waves upon the Gallic soil,
  The herald of his destiny.

XXXV.

Right loyal hearts about him beat
  Obedient to his royal will;
And Kentish bows were heard to twang,
  And swiftly cleaved the northern bill.

XXXVI.

And many a gallant cavalcade
  From *Cheshire*'s plains might now appear,
And many a proud and stalwart knight
  From *Lancashire* with shield and spear.

XXXVII.

The noble *Harry* turned his eye,
  With pride surveyed the numerous host ;
Not one but for his king would die,
  Nor make his loyalty a boast.

XXXVIII.

And now they come to *Agincourt*,
The Gallic foe appeared in view,
When quick the foremost ranks were thinned
As swift the clothyard arrows flew.

XXXIX.

On the French impetuous rush,
Seeking their English foes to crush ;
But each man with his henchman stood,
Nor ceased to strike till drained his blood.

XL.

Now backward hurtling to and fro,
The battle tide doth ebb and flow :
At length the Gallic foe give ground,
With English cheer the echoes sound.

XLI.

And where is *England's* king the while,
How bears the gallant *Harry* now ?
E'en in the thickest of the fight,
Around him many a fallen foe.

XLII. ·

And still he pressed his charger on,
And laid about him lustilie,
Yet had succumbed to whelming foes
But for the sword of *Percy Legh.*

XLIII.

His eagle eye the danger saw,
  And quick his towering form he threw
Before his liege—his upraised arm
  Swift the pressing foemen slew.

XLIV.

Still he maintained th' unequal fight,
  Till, by thronging bands o'erprest,
His life's blood welled from many a wound,
  And fainting drooped the ram's-head crest.

XLV.

' The king ! the king ! a rescue here ! '
  The English host was heard to cheer.
' Bear, guards, the bleeding knight away,
  His life to me and *England*'s dear.

XLVI.

' Tent him with care—for were it not
  That he were here, I had not been.
There beats not in this gallant host
  Than his a nobler heart, I ween.'

XLVII.

Then, breathing vengeance, sought again
  The king the Frenchmen's thickening host ;
They yielded soon on every side :
  England has won, and *France* has lost.

XLVIII.

Hotly the English host pursued
  Their vanquished foe for many a mile ;
But though it was a glorious day,
  The king was never seen to smile.

XLIX.

Quick he betook him to his tent,
  Resolved the wounded knight to see ;
And in deep sorrow o'er him bent—
  ' How is it with thee, *Percy Legh* ? '

L.

' Kind Heaven be praised that thou art here,
  And victory crowns the day at last ;
My gracious liege, my days are o'er,
  I feel my life blood ebbing fast.'

LI.

' Nay say not so my gallant knight,
  Thy king shall nurse thee tenderly ;
For thou didst save him in the fight,
  And he will give his love to thee.'

LII.

' A boon ! a boon ! my gracious liege,
  A boon I fain would ask of thee ;
I left at *Lyme* my fair young bride,
  Oh gently tent the Lady *Legh.*'

LIII.

They carried him to *Paris* town,
  They bore him there right carefully ;
But there he felt his strength was gone,
  And gently laid him down to die.

PART VII.

LIV.

Oh in that hour of utmost need,
  None *Blanche*'s unknown woes might heed ;
Nor think of her who wed despair
  When wed Sir *Piers* another fair.

LV.

They carried home his comely corse,
  To lay him with his ancestrie ;
And as they *Maxfield* forest pass,
  Sadly they think of Lady *Legh.*

LVI.

But the sad tidings *Blanche* first hears :
  One shriek she gave ! so wild and dread.
No word she spoke, she shed no tears ;
  Her hands pressed to her maddened head.

LVII.

They heaped above his corse a mound,
  A mound where now dark fir-trees wave ;
And moans at night are heard around
  From *Knight*'s *Lowe*, sweeping o'er the grave.

LVIII.

Blanche rambled all the night forlorn,
  Little she recked of wind and storm ;
And on the river's brink at morn
  Lay stiff in death her lovely form.

LIX.

They buried her where she was found,
  Where sadly sighs the *Bollin*'s wave ;
And ever since that meadow ground
  By all is called ' The Lady's Grave.'

Stanza 44. ' And fainting drooped the ram's-head crest.'   The crest of Legh of Lyme.

Stockport.

AMA refert Danos ubi nunc Stopporta locatur
Afflictos olim clade fuisse gravi ;
Inde urbi nomen, prædonum incursibus obex,
Quod datus hic Anglis sit quoque parta salus.

TRANSLATION.

In ages past the place where *Stopport* stands
Marked the repulse of hostile Danish bands ;
And thence according to the voice of fame,
The *Angles* safety gained, the town its name.

Stockport is still pronounced Stopport by its inhabitants. It has often been said hat the vulgar pronunciation often gives the clue to the origin and root of a name. So Frodsham is vulgarly pronounced Fordsham, i.e. the town of the ford. There is a tradition that the Danes were repulsed at Stockport, and the slain buried in a field below the castle, called the Park.

The Skeleton Hand.

I.

N old crone lived at *Lim* one day,
    Lim that is famed for best of hay;
    Water she scorned, or if, you see,
    She *water* drank, 'twas Eau de Vie.

II.

'Twas Eau de Vie : but when her hose
    She eke did wash, or other clothes,
    She scorned the brooklet in the vale,
    And at the church she filled her pail.

III.

She filled her pail at th' old church spout,
    In spite of neighbours who spoke out ;
    And said 'twas wrong her pail to fill
    At the church spout, and not the rill.

IV.

And not the rill: but though they talked,
    Her fancy would not thus be baulked ;
    She talked too, and swore ' that soft
    Water was best, she'd tried it oft.'

THE SKELETON HAND.

V.

She'd tried it oft. Once more she went
  To church, on sacrilege intent;
  The wild wind moaned, the torrents poured,
  The lightning flashed, the thunder roared.

VI.

The thunder roared, the gurgoyles grinned,
  The old crone trembled as she sinned;
  However that stupid she seemed,
  Lifted her pail, but sudden screamed.

VII.

But sudden screamed, for from the spout
  Which from the church tower stretched its snout
  Came a skeleton hand, and without fail
  Struck the old crone, and seized her pail.

VIII.

And seized her pail, as on her back
  She lay half stunned by sudden whack;
  She saw the hand and pail beside
  Through the thin lead pipe upwards glide.

IX.

She saw the pail through the thin pipe glide,
  Yet the pail was not crushed, nor its bands untied;
  Ne'er was the pail nor hand I ween
  By mortal eye again e'er seen.

X.

By mortal eye e'er seen: but she
Was found there, lying helplessly.
Some said 't was lightning, brandy some ;
They raised her up and took her home.

XI.

They took her home, and from that hour
She ne'er took a can to th' old church tower ;
Nought of the phantom hand she told
Save one dear friend she knew of old.

XII.

She knew of old, who swore that dumb
She'd ever prove, and not tell one ;
And not tell one—but she told two
Great friends, and thus the secret grew.

XIII.

The secret grew, and soon through *Lim*
Surged over and ran o'er the brim ;
Like lightning spread throughout the land
The crushed pail and skeleton hand.

MORAL.

Two things may all learn from this tale
Of the bone hand and th' old crone's pail ;
Go to the church your prayers to say,
Thence naught but good thoughts take away.

If there be aught you don't wish known,
Be sure to keep your counsel own ;
Else you may chance th' old proverb rue,
' Secret de trois, secret de tous.'

Lymm used to be spelt Lim—the correct spelling, from the root Limes, a boundary ; as the Mersey, which runs through Lim, divides Cheshire from Lancashire.

Stanza 1. 'Lim that is famed for best of hay.' 'To lick up a thing like Lim hay' is an old county proverb, expressive of superexcellence.

Stanza 6. 'However that stupid,' &c. ; 'that stoopid,' Cheshire for obstinate.

The French proverb, quoted in the last line, is in its entirety

Secret de deux, secret de Dieu ;
Secret de trois, secret de tous.

The Sands of *Dee.*

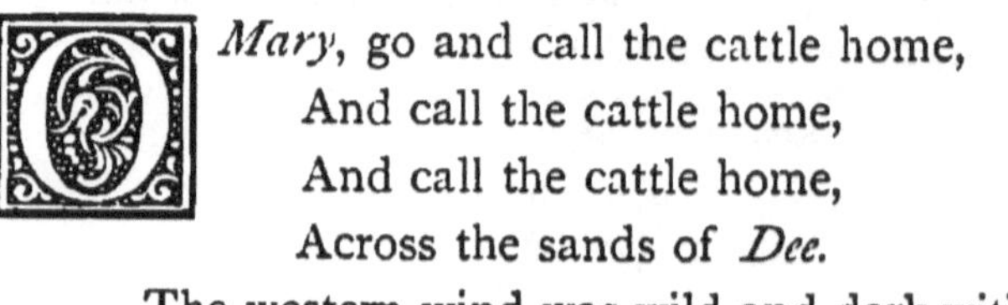

Mary, go and call the cattle home,
 And call the cattle home,
 And call the cattle home,
 Across the sands of *Dee.*
The western wind was wild and dark with foam,
 And all alone went she.

The western tide crept up along the sand,
 And o'er and o'er the sand,
 And round and round the sand,
 As far as the eye could see.
The rolling mist swept down, and hid the land,
 And never home came she !

O is it weed, or fish, or floating hair?
 A tress of golden hair,
 A drowned maiden's hair,
 Above the nets at sea ;
Was never salmon yet that shone so fair
 Among the stakes at *Dee.*

They rowed her in across the rolling foam,
The cruel crawling foam,
The cruel hungry foam,
To her grave beside the sea !
But still the boatmen hear her call her cattle home
Across the sands of *Dee.*

The author of the above, which has been set to music, is the Rev. Charles Kingsley, Rector of Winchfield, the last male representative of the Kingsleys of Kingsley.

Epitaph on an Old *Chester* Woman
who sold Pottery.

BENEATH this stone lies *Catherine Gray*,
Changed to a lifeless lump of clay ;
By earth and clay she got her pelf,
Yet now she's turned to earth itself.
Ye weeping friends, let me advise,
Abate your grief and dry your eyes,
For what avail a flood of tears :
Who knows but in a run of years,
In some tall pitcher or broad pan,
She in her shop may be again.

The Wishing Steps.

A Legend of Chester.

[Near the south-east corner of the city walls at Chester, and forming part of the Wall, and as you turn northwards, are a flight of steps called 'The Wishing Steps.' The *religio loci* is, that whatever wish may be formed at the bottom of these steps will, in the course of time, be surely fulfilled, provided the wisher can run to the top and back again without drawing breath. Another version is that the aspirant must not only go up and down, but up again; but those who have been *once* up and down will prefer the double to the treble transit, and find even then their task is not easy unless gifted with the lungs of a pearl-diver, as there are six flights of three steps each, with a landing of five feet between each flight. St. John's tower, Beeston castle, and the river Dee are the principal objects from this spot.]

I.

AH! many a youth and maid each year
    Have here raced up and down,
Panting with speed of mountain deer,
    Some long-formed wish to crown.

II.

And there are those whose oft crost lot
    Hopes here may balm receive,
Mistrust the legend of the spot,
    And yet would fain believe.

III.

Though wild perchance that legend be,
    And though the tale be vain,
Grudge not the wretch in misery
    What bids him hope again.

IV.

Some climb by dark revenge distraught,
  Or fierce resolve of hate,
Some, laughing, *feign* to mount in sport,
  Yet hope to bind their fate.

V.

One morn I marked a beauteous maid
  'The Wishing Steps' draw nigh.
She paused—I felt a prayer was said :
  Her bosom heaved a sigh.

VI.

She gazed not on the hallowed *Dee*,
  That rolls beneath the Wall ;
For *Beeston*'s heights no thought had she,
  The Wish was all in all.

VII.

The telltale blush, the long-drawn sigh
  (The thought from all concealed),
The eloquence of downcast eye,
  To me that wish revealed.

VIII.

Unspoke I could that thought divine :
  'Oh may I be his bride !
This granted ; the whole world is mine.
  Wish I have none beside.'

IX.

Then up she sprang with angel grace ;
 I watched her swift return—
Swift as *Camilla* in the race,
 Who topped th' unbending corn.

X.

And when she panting drew her breath,
 I saw a happy smile :
Ever the heart, till chilled by death,
 Wishes, hope fed, beguile.

Stanza 6. 'She gazed not on the hallowed Dee.' In Milton we find, 'or ancient hallowed Dee.' Randolph, in his poems, also notices 'the holy Dee.'

The Iron Gates.

A Legend of Alderley.

THE writhing mists of autumn's sky
    Still hid the heights of *Alderley*,
    And scarlet leaves fell thick and fast,
    In dragon forms the dim clouds past,
And scarce the sun, in feeble ray,
Broke through the gloom with tardy day;
Bowed to the breeze the pine-tree swung,
And dewdrops on each blackthorn hung :
Just such a scene as those appalling
Who (ventured in some homebred calling),
Some chance hath brought to heath and plains,
And splashing moors and falling rains;
Then memory turns to smoke and strife,
And screaming bairns and scolding wife,
And noise and strife seem fair and good
Compared with such wild solitude.
But other thoughts employed the mind
Of yon rough-coated Cestrian hind;
He, bred in scenes where winter's cold
Has early made each urchin bold,
Heeds not the blast, the miry way,
The falling leaf, the sullen day,

But eager posting to the fair,
With armèd heel spurred on his mare.
A flowing mane, his favourite steed
(Pride of his grandsire's fav'rite breed)
Graced the smooth neck and ample chest,
And this his early care had drest;
For 'tis the pride, the *Cestrian*'s brag,
The bone and breeding of his nag:
He loved his nag, yet sighed for gold,
He wished her kept, he wished her sold.
So have I seen temptation even
Within my chapel wall, St. *Stephen* !
Where some great patriot would retain
The mob's loud plaudit but for gain;
Now much in doubt for glory burns,
And now towards the Premier turns;
Conquered at last by love of gold,
And, like the farmer's nag, is sold.
　　Strong blew the breeze with whistling rain,
His hat fell flapping o'er his face,
A moment checked the farmer's pace,
When right before his horse's head
A dark huge figure seemed to spread.
The startled mare pricked up each ear,
The farmer's hair stood up for fear,
As straight before his purposed road
A huge black monster's vast form strode.
Above the human height it seemed,
Bright lightning from his eyeballs gleamed,
And from beneath the shadowy brow
A solemn voice spoke deep and low:—

‘ Stranger, attend ! and traveller, hear !
I know what business brought you here ;
I know thy errand, and full well
Thy sordid purpose can I tell—
Thou’dst give thy favourite mare for pelf,
And sell for little more thyself ;
But know, thy horse is doomed to be
Heir to a nobler destiny :
Sell as thou wilt that steed of thine,
’Tis fated that the steed be mine.
Yet go ; though I can ne’er deceive,
Thy stubbornness will ne’er believe ;
Mix with the chapmen all, and try
Who chaffers for her, who will buy :—
A vain attempt, but be it so,
And to the purposed market go.
But mark me well ; ’tis my behest
That when the sun sinks in the West,
And e’er the moon with silver light
Shall make yon waving pine-tree bright,
Return thou here, and bring thy steed :
Fear not *if* here, else fear indeed.
Go ponder on my firm behest,
But mark the hour, and watch the West.’
The warning ceased ; the *Cestrian*’s eye
Gazed,—but it gazed on vacancy !
For man nor seeming man was there—
All was dissolved, and nought but air,
And sky, and hill, and heath, and wood,
Where late the wizard form had stood.

He gasped for breath, with terror cold,
But soon aroused, for he was bold
By nature—and to such is light
The strongest image of affright.
To his good steed he gave the rein,
And swiftly scudded o'er the plain,
Reached in an hour the busy scene
Where the crowd thickened on the green—
The village green.   The gathering crowd,
In festive mirth, or bickerings loud,
The tempting baits in order spread :
The husband gilt in gingerbread,
The lowing calf in crowded pen,
The tiger roaring in his den.
All that can please, amuse, amaze,
Broke on the *Cestrian*'s gladdened gaze.
The swinging bush, high hung in air,
Proclaimed good ale was selling there ;
High on a booth, with clattering din,
Stood grinning clown and harlequin ;
And cunning men of fate full sure,
And quacks infallible to cure.
Pleased, though not wildered with the scene,
Thrift and pleasure placed between,
The *Cestrian*, though he liked it well,
Was come for profit, and to sell.
   Up through the street the snow-white mare
Sped her best pace—a trotter rare ;
Beneath her feet the pavement burned
As in a gallop she returned ;

Then, standing up on rising ground,
Swift and sure he warrants sound.
Some praised, and some found fault; the same,
For still no real bidder came.
'For guineas! Pounds! I'll give one back.
For road, for harness, such a hack!'
Yet still no buyer came.   The sun
Proclaimed his daily race was run;
And now he thought of the behest
By the gay gilding in the West.
He must not pause, for now full soon
Will rise and shine the silver moon.
He must obey.   Bound by that spell,
He bade the noisy crowd farewell;
Returning with less eager pace,
(Not without fear) regained the place—
The place where late the phantom stood,
Half way between the hill and wood.
Oft his mind turned upon the cause,
Why Nature broke her common laws;
Why she allowed, by day or night,
To wander thus th' imprisoned sprite.
His cheek now flushed, now icy cold
Turnèd by chance, by nature bold.
Seven lofty firs had marked the spot,
Which *Cestrians* since have ne'er forgot,
And there, upon the thymy green
Reclined, the wizard form was seen,
Beneath a rock of summit steep
Lay the wrapped warner as in sleep.

The rider paused with tightened rein,
Viewed the strange sleeper o'er again,
Taxed his own timid heart, and said,
' I have no sense of guilt ; and dread
To guilt belongs. My arm is strong ;
Then to the base such fears belong.
Up and be bold ! and fairly boast
Thy first encounter with a ghost.'
He spurred his steed, and nearer drew,
But as he came more near in view
Of that same form of unknown evil,
(That unsubstantial, might-be devil),
His shivering fit returned, and charms
He thought on for all magic harms :
Beads had he none, and little skill
To muster up a prayer at will ;
And once a sense of deep affright
To ebbing courage counselled flight.
But to cut short his meditation,
The phantom took his former station,
And right before his horse's head
The giant form again was spread.
' 'Tis well,' he said, ' good man and true ;
Now follow me, and take thy due.'
And down the sable phantom strode,
With noiseless step, the northern road ;
The leafless wood they passed beneath,
And crossed upon the dreary heath ;
By *Stormy Point* where tempests roll,
They pass, and next by *Saddle Boll.*

The horseman paused, and seemed to say,
Here stand !—no further will I stray !
E'en at this instant, from the ground
Forth issuing, came a hollow sound.
Now sank indeed the *Cestrian*'s soul,
Back on his heart the pulses roll,
For now appeared his sable guide
In all the stern magician's pride,
And to the farmer's startled sight
He seemed to swell in form and height.
Loose from his form his vesture flowed,
His piercing eye with fury glowed,
And when he muttering breathed a spell,
Earth trembling yawned, and seeming hell,
With all the very worst of fates,
Stood opening by two IRON GATES !
He waved his hand, and as he spake,
Earth to its centre 'gan to quake.
Now plunged the steed, and on the ground
Soon was th' affrighted rider found,
Who, kneeling at th' enchanter's feet,
In piteous tones did thus entreat :—
' Oh, mighty chief of magic spell !
Art thou not pledged to treat me well ?
Didst thou not promise my return
My safety from thy charms should earn ? '
' It shall do so ;—be bold, proceed,
I'll stay thee at thy utmost need.
Be bold, and enter ; feast thy eye
With more than mortal scrutiny.'

E'en at the word a spreading cave
(Such as the Alpine hermits have)
Sudden appeared with opening wide.
Bright from the roof on every side
Hang pendent crystals, icy, bright,
Reflecting back phosphoric light ;
Unsteady vapours seemed to play
A sort of intermitting day.
Entered yet deeper, to the walls
Were fixed innumerable stalls,
Where milk-white coursers, side by side,
(Just like his own) were careful tied,
And close by every steed was found
An armèd man, in slumber bound ;
And more and more the numbers seemed,
As up the vault the vapours gleamed.
Bright was each steed from heel to hoof,
Bright was each blade of temper proof,
And *Mars* himself, with prideful eye,
Had viewed such host of cavalry.
Further they passed ; in clefts of rock
Was stored bright gold, a plenteous stock,
But deeper hid within the gloom
There stood in this sepulchral room
A mighty chest of ponderous size,
Bolted with bands of many dies.
Up to this chest th' enchanter came,
And brighter burned his magic flame ;
And as he turned the massive lock,
The echo rang from rock to rock.

Then from the chest with care he told
To the bold *Cestrian* counted gold.
' The steed is mine; bid wonder cease ;
Receive thy gold, depart in peace.'
' Nay ; tell me more !' the *Cestrian* cried ;
' Why are these steeds in order tied ?
Why sleep those men all bright in arms ?
And why prepared for war's alarms ?
Say, are they doomed to mortal toil,
Or destined to unearthly broil ?'
On this the wizard changed his face,
Assumed a mild and brighter grace,
And to his tone was something given
As from a messenger from heaven.
' These are the Caverned Troops—by fate
Foredoomed the guardians of our state.
England's good genius here detains
These armèd defenders of her plains ;
Doomed to remain till that dread day
When foemen, marshalled in array,
And fiends intestine shall combine
To seal the ruin of our line.
Thrice lost shall *England* be, thrice won,
'Twixt dawn of day and setting sun ;
Then we, the wondrous CAVERNED BAND !
These mailèd martyrs for the land,
Shall rush resistless on the foe,
And they the power of *Cestrians* know ;
And thus all-glorious day be won
By royal *George*, great *George*'s son.

Then bootless groans shall travellers hear,
Who pass thy forest, *Delamere*!
Their dabbled wings shall ravens toss,
 Croaking o'er bloodstained *Headless Cross*.
But peace!—May be another age
Shall write these records on her page.
Begone!'—Nor dared the farmer wait;
In haste he past the IRON GATES.
He heard the bolts descend and clash,
And the hills echoed to the crash.
He turned to gaze;—his searching eye
Found nothing round save earth and sky.
Wondering he stands, but fears to stay,
Homeward in haste pursues his way.
Soon was the strange adventure told
To what high fate his horse was sold;
The neighbours hasten to the spot,
Vainly they search, they find it not.
No trace remained; nor since that night
Hath mortal eye beheld the sight,
And till the hour decreed by fate
None shall e'er see the IRON GATE.

The Unfortunate Loves of *Thomas Clutterbuck* and *Polly Higginbotham.*

A Broadside.

I.

N *Chester* town a man there dwelt,
Not rich as *Crœsus*, but a buck ;
The pangs of love he dearly felt,
His name was *Thomas Clutterbuck.*
The ladye he did most approve
Most guineas gold had got 'em,
And *Clutterbuck* fell deep in love
With *Polly Higginbotham.*
    Oh, *Thomas Clutterbuck !*
    And oh, *Polly Higginbotham !*
I sing the loves, the smiling loves,
Of *Clutterbuck* and *Polly Higginbotham.*

II.

A little trip he did propose,
Upon the *Dee* they got 'em ;
The wind blew high, he blew his nose,
And sang to *Polly Higginbotham.*

The strain was sweet, the stream was deep !
He thought his notes had caught her ;
But she, alas ! first fell asleep,
And then fell, in the water !
    Oh, *Polly Higginbotham !*
    She went to the bottom.
I sing the death, the doleful death,
Of pretty *Polly Higginbotham.*

III.

Yet still he strained his little throat,
To love he did invite her,
And never missed until his boat,
He thought, went rather lighter ;
But when he saw that she was gone,
The summum of his wishes,
He boldly paid the waterman;
And jumped among the fishes.
    Oh, *Polly Higginbotham !*
    He comes to the bottom.
I sing the death, the double death,
Of *Clutterbuck* and *Higginbotham.*

IV.

Round *Chester* stalk, the river ghosts
Of this young man and fair maid ;
His head looks like a salmon-trout,
Her tail is like a mermaid.

Learn this, ye constant lovers all,
Who live in *England*'s island,
The way to shun a wat'ry death
Is making love on dry land !
    Oh, *Polly Higginbotham !*
    Who lies at the bottom.
I sing the ghosts, the wat'ry ghosts,
Of *Clutterbuck* and *Higginbotham*.

Cheshire Wyches.

[Printed for the benefit of the Northwich Bazaar, 1840.]

I.

THE 'Wyches,' and their plenteous store
Of rock-salt and of brine,
I sing,—a theme unsung before
By any lyre but mine.

II.

Apollo ! thou the song exalt,
And from *Parnassus* mine
Impregnate with true Attic salt
This rhapsody saline.

III.

Our 'Wyches' if deprived of these,
No salt below the soil,
In vain to thrutch the daily cheese
Would *Cheshire* damsel toil.

IV.

In infancy we all were taught
 A trick that never fails,
How easily old birds are caught
 With salt upon their tails.

V.

A salmon hooked from fin to fin,
 Full fifteen inches wide,
A pretty pickle he'd be in,
 Were *Cheshire* salt denied !

VI.

When fattened hogs, of life bereft,
 The appetite awaken,
What recipe have housewives left,
 Save salt, to save their bacon ?

VII.

Oude, skilled in soups and fricandeaux,
 Without it were at fault,
Himself unequal to compose
 A substitute for salt.

VIII.

Soupe maigre were more maigre still,
 Cold salads, grass would be ;—
Eat devils without salt who will,
 The devil a bit for me !

IX.

No omen sad to cause alarm,
  The mustard-pot o'erthrown ;
Nor threatens any future harm
  When pepper falls alone.

X.

But salt, if spilt, each guest shall rue ;
  The scattered grains foretell
Bad luck to him who overthrew,
  And worse to whom it fell.

XI.

Fair *Venus*, rising from the sea,
  Was born upon the tide ;
This charming goddess, what was she
  But salt personified ?

XII.

To her, the queen of smiles and mirth,
  Old Ocean's loveliest daughter,
Nor fount nor river stream gave birth,
  No—salt was in the water.

XIII.

As in the sea so on the strand
  Its properties combine,
And *Cheshire* is the favoured land
  Of Beauty and of Brine.

XIV.

This nation may our queen exalt,
  And blessings still accrue,
And never may one tear of salt
  The royal eye bedew.

XV.

When knaves and traitors she would clear
  From foul corruption's blot,
We'll bathe them, if she sends them here,
  In brine-pan boiling hot.

XVI.

If *France* has not had war enough,
  We're ready still to meet her;
And give our foe a pinch of snuff
  In the shape of black saltpetre.

XVII.

Salt Hill invites the world to share
  The Montem's festive scene;
For ages salt and silver there
  Synonymous have been.

XVIII.

Since all who deal in salt have skill
  As *Midas* had of old,
May salt to-day our coffers fill,
  And ev'ry grain be gold.

THE MONK AND LADY.

The Lady's Shelf.

A legend of Hilbree Island.

I.

N islet rises from the waves
    Where *Deva* weds the sea ;
Its shores fresh and salt water laves :
    The isle is called *Hilbree.*

II.

There is a cave with pink flowers dight
    (Bairns ' Lady Cushions ' call) ;
Hence you may gaze on ocean's might,
    Far grandest scene of all.

III.

The grotto's y'clept the ' Lady's Cave,'
    A ledge of rock behind
The ' Lady's Shelf ' is named, by wave
    Spray lashed and eke by wind.

IV.

Fond youth and maidens fair meet there,
    To while a summer's hour ;
And laughter gay, and merry cheer,
    Oft ring through rocky bower.

v.

Little they reck that in this grot
   A monk his beads once told !—
That to that shelf, that very spot,
   The waves a maid's corse rolled !

vi.

List, ladies ! list ! whilst I unfold
   Of love and woe a mine ;
At *Hilbree* Isle watched monks of old
   St. *Hildeburgha*'s shrine.

vii.

A Benedictine monk with toil
   Here hollowed out a cave ;
And here alone would come to foil
   Satan or watch the wave.

viii.

One e'en he sought his loved retreat,
   When on that shelf he saw
A beauteous maid pale as a sheet
   Bespurpled o'er with gore.

ix.

Rich was the vesture she had on,
   Though stained and dank with wet ;
A carcanet of jewels shone
   Amidst her tresses jet.

X.

Sudden he flew to seek some aid,
  (Should life's chain be unbroke);
When a weak voice his footsteps stayed,
  And thus the maiden spoke :

XI.

' Stay, father, stay, a daughter shrive,
  Whose time on earth is short :
The moments wane I 've yet to live,—
  Oh ! I am sore distraught.

XII.

' A knightly pennon floats abroad,
  From *Shotwyke*'s turrets high,
Of *Shotwyke*'s tower my sire is lord,
  His only daughter—I.

XIII.

' Save me, he child had none beside ;
  Ne'er knew I mother's care ;
For young and beautiful she died
  The hour that me she bare.

XIV.

' Edgar alone, my father's esquire
  (He was an orphan boy),
Brother and sister was, my sire
  With me loved him to toy.

XV.

' 'T was he my merlin from its nest
Reclaimed and tamed for me ;
Zealous, forestalled my least behest,
And where I went—was he.

XVI.

' My bark upset where deep's the wave ;
'T was Edgar's ready hand
That drew me from a watery grave,
And brought me safe to land.

XVII.

' A robber band in ambush lay,
And carried me away ;
'T was Edgar's chance their chief to slay,
And snatch me from the fray.

XVIII.

At dead of night the crackling fire
Wrapped round my sleeping bower ;
'T was Edgar scaled the burning pyre,
And bore me from the tower.

XIX.

' Edgar was tall and strong, his hair
Curled o'er his forehead broad;
First in the chace, and first in war,
He looked of all the lord.

XX.

‘ Cunning in gentler arts of peace,
    The song, the tale, the lyre,
He knew my maiden heart to please,
    And felt a kindred fire.

XXI.

‘ We loved—’t is an old tale ! yes, we
    Loved, yet ne’er spoke of love :
Unfelt, it came all noislessly,
    Like feathers on the dove.

XXII.

‘ We dreamt—Alas how changed the scene
    This happiness must last,
The future ’d prove as erst had been
    Our present to our past.

XXIII.

‘ Not long the calm—in summer hour,
    The thunder’s roll we hear,
When not a sigh floats through the air
    The hurricane is near.

XXIV.

‘ A Welsh knight came, by rumour famed,
    He sought my father’s side ;
His blood, his wealth, his love proclaimed,
    And prayed me for his bride.

XXV.

' My sire the wished-for promise past,
    Too easy was he wiled,
With noble lord in wedlock fast
    To bind his only child.

XXVI.

' Instant he sought my bower—well pleased,
    Exulting, told his tale ;
My sinking frame confusion seized,
    I turned as spectre pale.

XXVII.

' Long had I lived in fancy's maze,
    The truth now flashed out bright ;
I felt with one I'd pass my days—
    That one, was not the Knight.

XXVIII.

' Too soon my proud sire learnt the cause
    Why I the stranger fled ;
He threatened sore, but nature's laws
    Were not to be gainsaid.

XXIX.

' The drawbridge fell, *Llewellyn*'s steed
    Away my suitor bears :
I felt as when in straitest need
    A wretch his respite hears.

PART II.

XXX.

‘ “ *Gertrude*,” one morn my father cried,
   “ Thy bravest kirtle don,
With an old friend, before next tide,
   We ’ll spend some hours anon.”

XXXI.

‘ Soon we embarked ; our shallop flew,
   Brightly the sunbeams played ;
What fate prepared I little knew—
   Alas, I was betrayed !

XXXII.

‘ As our bark neared the *Point of Air*,
   Sternly my father said,
“ *Gertrude*, thy fate is sealed—to share
   As bride *Llewellyn*’s bed.

XXXIII.

‘ “ This e’en the marriage-party meet,
   The vassals throng around ;
The daughter of a Knight ’t is meet
   Should a Knight’s bride be found.

XXXIV.

‘ “ In vain you now for *Edgar* grieve,
   That love-sick boy I ’ve found
A bridal couch he ’ll never leave—
   The ocean depths profound.”

XXXV.

' I heard of hated spousals near,
  And shuddered as he spoke ;
I felt no fear, I shed no tear,
  Although my heart was broke.

XXXVI.

' But when he told of *Edgar*'s death,
  Fainting I sank on deck ;
Light left mine eyes, my fleeting breath
  Escaped my body's wreck.

XXXVII.

' I felt as if all round was dark,
  I thought (as in a dream)
A sudden surge swept o'er the bark
  And whelmed me in its stream.

XXXVIII.

' Methought I heard my father's voice
  Cry frantic—" Save my child—
Edgar still lives ! if he 's thy choice
  He 's mine—my child ! my child ! "

XXXIX.

' The waters wild my frame upbore,
  Bechilled by beating wave ;
A dreadful shock—I felt no more
  Till wakened in this cave.   -

XL.

'My ebbing pulse foretells my doom.
  Strip off each bridal gem;
Wed my cold body to the tomb,
  And sing my requiem.

XLI.

'Tell *Edgar* I 've been sorely tried,
  'That with my latest breath—'
She ceased—the monk looked up and sighed,
  He felt that it was—Death.

XLII.

Pink flowers still deck that rocky bower
  In beauty, as of old;
But never monk there, from that hour,
  His beads hath ever told.

XLIII.

The *Dee* and *Wave* their floods entwine,
  As they had done of yore;
But famed St. *Hildeburgha*'s shrine
  Cowled fathers watch no more.

Stanza 2. 'Bairns Lady Cushions call;' this is the popular name for the Sea Thrift, or Pink, which grows in profusion on Hilbree Island. Hilbree Island belongs to the parish of St. Oswald of Chester, though distant twenty miles.

The Souler's Song.

[The Soulers, on All Souls' Eve, go from door to door 'Souling,' i.e. singing, drinking, and begging. It is a remnant of the popish superstition of praying at that particular season for departed souls. All Souls' Day is set apart in many Roman Catholic countries for the living to visit the graves of their departed friends and relations.]

I.

YE gentlemen of *England*, I would have ye draw near
To these few lines which we have wrote, and which
   you soon shall hear,
Sweet melody of music all on this evening clear,
For we are come a souling for apples and strong beer.

II.

Step down into your cellar, and see what you can find ;
If your barrels are not empty, I hope you will prove kind ;
I hope you will prove kind with your apples and strong beer,
We 'll come no more a souling until another year.

III.

Cold winter, it is coming on, dark, dirty, wet, and cold ;
To try your goodnature this night we do make bold ;
This night we do make bold with your apples and strong beer ;
We will come no more a souling until another year.

IV.

All the houses we 've been at we 've had both meat and drink,
So now we 're dry with travelling, I hope you 'll on us think.
I hope you 'll on us think, with your apples and strong beer,
And we 'll come no more a souling until another year.

V.

God bless the master of this house, and the mistress also ;
And all the little children that round the table go ;
Likewise your men and maidens, your cattle, and your store,
And all that lies within your gates, we wish you ten times more.
We wish you ten times more, with your apples and strong beer,
For we 'll come no more a souling until another year.

Quæsitum Meritis.

[At the Annual Tarporley Hunt Meeting, all toasts considered worthy of the honour are drunk in a Quæsitum, a name given to particular glasses from the inscription they bear—
' Quæsitum Meritis.']

I.

A CLUB of good fellows, we meet once a year,
    When the leaves of the forest are yellow and sear;
    By the motto that shines in each glass it is shown
    We pledge in our cups the deserving alone.
Our glass a Quæsitum, ourselves *Cheshire* men,
May we fill it and drink it again and again.

II.

We hold in abhorrence all Vulpicide knaves,
With their guns and their traps, and their velveteen slaves;
They may feed their fat pheasants, their foxes destroy,
And mar the prime sport they themselves can't enjoy;
But such sportsmen as these we good fellows condemn,
And I vow we 'll ne'er drink a Quæsitum to them.

III.

That man of his wine is unworthy indeed
Who grudges to mount a poor fellow in need;
Who keeps for nought else but to purge them with balls,
Like a dog in a manger, his nags in their stalls;
Such niggards as these we good fellows condemn,
And I vow we 'll ne'er drink a Quæsitum to them.

IV.

Some riders there are who, too jealous of place,
Will fling back a gate in their next neighbour's face ;
Some never pull up when a friend gets a fall ;
Some ride over friends, hounds, horses, and all ;
Such riders as these we good fellows condemn,
And I vow we 'll ne'er drink a Quæsitum to them.

V.

For coffee-house gossip some hunters come out,
Of all matters prating save that they're about :
From scandal and cards they to politics roam,
They ride forty miles, head the fox, and go home !
Such sportsmen as these we good fellows condemn,
And I vow we 'll ne'er drink a Quæsitum to them.

VI.

Since one fox on foot more diversion will bring
Than twice twenty thousand cock pheasants on wing,
That man we all honour, whatever his rank,
Whose heart heaves a sigh when his gorse is drawn blank.
Quæsitum ! quæsitum ! fill up to the brim,
We 'll drink if we die for 't, a bumper to him.

VII.

O give me that man to whom nought comes amiss,
One horse or another, that country or this,
Through falls and bad starts who undauntedly still
Rides up to this motto, ' Be with 'em I will.'
Quæsitum ! quæsitum ! fill up to the brim ;
We 'll drink if we die for 't, a bumper to him.

VIII.

Oh give me that man who can ride through a run,
Nor engross to himself all the glory when done ;
Who calls not each horse that o'ertakes him a 'screw,'
Who loves a run best when a friend sees it too !
Quæsitum ! quæsitum ! fill up to the brim,
We 'll drink if we die for 't, a bumper to him.

IX.

Oh give me that man who himself goes the pace,
And whose table is free to all friends of the chase :
Should a spirit so choice in this wide world be seen,
He rides, you may swear, in a collar of green.
Quæsitum ! quæsitum ! fill up to the brim,
We 'll drink if we die for 't, a bumper to him.

I heard an old Cheshire sportsman assert vehemently that he would sooner have written the above song than the ' Annals ' of Tacitus.—E. L.

The Two Rectors.

A tale of Malpas.

[To explain the Cheshire proverb ‘Higgledy Piggledy Malpas shot, let every tub stand on its own bottom.’]

'TWAS once on a time—’T is the regular way
A tale to begin, should one have ought to say ;
’T was once on a time—I repeat it again,
Some great king (like Haroun Al Raschid) was
fain
To see for himself what things passed in his realm ;
I don’t know his name, if I knew it I’d tell ’m ;
’T was *Edgar* perhaps, or possibly *Guillelm*—
His name never mind—though I am not of those
Who could for one instant be brought to suppose,
If toadstool ’t were named, I could fancy a rose
Would equally please a fastidious nose.
I can’t think that *Barbara*, *Cicely*, or *Peggy*,
That *Dowse*, *Joan*, *Dorothy*, *Lettice*, or *Meggy*,
Can have such sweet faces as *Gertrude* or *Blanche*,
Or others in whose praises fain I would launch ;
But I won’t mention more, for in *Cheshire* the beauties
Are so many in number, that one poet’s duties
Would hardly suffice to enumerate all
The names of those ladies whom lovely we call

The King, in his wanderings, to *Malpas* chance came,
A picturesque town with an ill-omened name.
He went to the inn—whether *Angel* or *Crown*
Is not said—but conclude 't was the best in the town.
He called for the landlord, and ordered of ale
A large humming tankard, at once, without fail;
Then went to the taproom, where, sipping their beer,
Sat Rector and Curate, enjoying good cheer.
The parsons he joined, who indeed did not know then
(Incognito kings are so very like low men)
That a king had come in—for never a king
Had before come to *Malpas*; in short, 't was a thing
That th' oldest inhabitant (oft-quoted being)
Could not to his memory in any shape bring.
The Rector was fat—I would lay you a bet,
That 'mongst all his songs he 'd not ' Dinna forget ;'
In short, a man he was fond of his dinner.
Who's not ?   The Curate was visibly thinner.
Thick as thieves they became, and past a pleasant night;
Talked over the times—not the *Times* of this day,
For then e'en the *Times* was not published, they say.
Thus, Rector enlightened, the King got a sight
Of what, hitherto, he 'd been ignorant quite ;
What the talk of the town—the poor—price of flour—
What was said of himself.   The King in one hour
Had then more etcæteras brought to his ears
Than he'd heard at court in twice as many years.
All things have an end— they had talked, drunk, and fed,
And thought now 't was time all to toddle to bed ;
They call for the bill, a serious total—
Hot suppers, Welsh rabbits, six brandies, and ale.

The King saw the Curate most visibly quail,
And, shivering, turn for a moment quite pale,
As, sighing, it struck him a third of that bill
Must come from a purse could afford it but ill.
Says the King to the Rector, ' Come, let us stand treat.'
' No, no,' quoth the Rector, ' that would not be reeght;
You've ne'er heard our *Malpas* old proverb, I wot ;
It is " Higgledy Piggledy *Malpas* shot ; "
Which means, that with us when a man drinks his beer,
He must not think others must pay for his cheer.'
Quoth the King, ' *Maxfield* measure (I think) " heap and
    thrutch,"
Is a *Cheshire* proverb than yours better much ;
For this *is* a generous notion, whilst yours
A mean excuse is for a most shabby course ;
Come, let's pay his shot, if you'll take counsel mine,
You may some day say it is better than thine.
Remember ! " A stitch in time sometimes saves nine." '
The Rector was stupid ; the King paid the shot
For self and the Curate, who, pleased with his lot,
Wished doubtless the stranger for rector he 'd got.
Next morn came an Edict—the Rector to vex :
It began —To all greeting—ended, Vivat Rex.
Joint Rector it made the thin Curate.   Besides,
Half glebe, half offerings, and half of the tithes.
What the new Rector gained the old Rector lost,
Which the latter soon found out too true to his cost.
The cause of the sad change he could not divine,
Till, startling, he thought ' A stitch in time saves nine ! '

He shivered and shrank, when it burst on his mind,
It must be the King! with whom last night I dined.
He cursed '*Malpas* shot,' but too late he repined.
From that time the King had thus settled the matter,
Th' old Rector grew thinner, the new one grew fatter.
From that day to this the case always has been
Two Rectors at *Malpas* together are seen.

Line 21. 'An ill-omened name,' Mal-pas.—Line 61. 'Maxfield measure.' Maxfield or Macclesfield measure, 'heap and thrutch,' is a local proverb implying full, generous, over-flowing measure. In a Cheshire May song occurs the following incitement to generosity:

Give every one two and above.
The more you do give the more you will have,
And God will you certainly love.

Line 56. 'That would not be reeght,' Cheshire for *right*. In an address of part of the Chester grand jury to Sir J. Jekyl, about 1710 (versified), we find the following line:

Reeght natural spriggs of the Rump Parliament.

There are two rectors at Lymn as well as at Malpas; but in the former town there is no traditionary royal visit or any reason, indeed, to account for it. A pleasant story concerning the name of Malpas we find in Giraldus Cambrensis. 'It happened in our times that a certain Jew, travelling towards Shrewsbury with the Archdeacon of this place whose name was Peche (i.e. Sin), and the Dean who was called Devel, and hearing the Archdeacon say that his Archdeaconry began at a place called "Ill Street" and reached as far as Malpas (Mal-pas) towards Chester,—the Jew, knowing both their names, told them very pleasantly, "He found it would be a miracle if ever he got safe out of this county; and his reason was, because Sin was the Archdeacon, and the Devil was the Dean; and, moreover, because the entry into the Archdeaconry was Ill Street, and the going forth again Mal-pas."'

Ode on Vale Royal.

[Written by Warton, probably about the middle of the 18th century.]

I.

S evening slowly spreads her mantle hoar,
   No ruder sounds the bounded valley fill
Than the faint din from yonder sedgy shore
   Of rushing waters and the murmuring mill.

II.

How sunk the scene where cloistered leisure mused !
  Where war-worn *Edward* paid his awful vow,
And, lavish of magnificence, diffused
  His crowded spires o'er the broad mountain's brow.

III.

The golden fans (that o'er the turret strown,
   Quick glancing to the sun, wild music made,)
Are reft, and ev'ry battlement o'ergrown
   With knotted thorns and the tall sapling's shade.

IV.

The prickly thistle sheds its plumy crest,
   And matted nettles shade the crumbling mass,
Where shone the pavement's surface smooth imprest,
   With rich reflection of the storied glass.

v.

Here hardy chieftains slept in proud repose,
   Sublimely shrined in glorious imagery;
And through the lessening aisles in radiant rows
   Their consecrated banners hung on high.

vi.

There oxen browse, and there the sable yew
   Through the dim void displays its baleful glooms,
And sheds in lingering drops unwholesome dew
   O'er the forgotten graves and scattered tombs.

vii.

By the slow clock in stately measured chime,
   That from the massy tower tremendous tolled,
No more the ploughman counts the tedious time,
   Nor distant shepherd pens his twilight fold.

viii.

High o'er the trackless heath, at midnight seen,
   No more the windows ranged in long array,
(Where the tall shaft, and fretted nook between
   Thick ivy twines) the tapered rights betray.

ix.

E'en now, amidst the wavering ivy wreaths
   (While kindred thoughts the pensive sounds inspire),
When the weak breeze in many a whisper breathes,
   I seem to listen to the chanting quire.

X.

As o'er these shattered towers intent we muse,
    Though reared by charity's capricious zeal ;
Yet can our breasts soft pity's sigh refuse ?
    Or conscious candour's modest plea conceal ?

XI.

For though the sorceress (Superstition blind),
    Amid the pomp of dreadful sacrifice,
O'er the dim roofs, to cheat the trancèd mind,
    Oft made her visionary gleams arise ;

XII.

Though the vain hours unsocial sloth beguiled,
    Whilst the still cloister's gate oblivion locked ;
And through the chambers pale, to slumbers mild
    Wan Indolence her drowsy cradle rocked ;

XIII.

Yet hence, enthroned in venerable state,
    Proud Hospitality dispensed her store.
Ah see beneath yon towers' unvaulted gate,
    Forlorn she sits upon the brambled floor !

XIV.

Her ponderous vase, with Gothic portraiture
    Embossed, no more with balmy moisture flows ;
Mid the mix'd shards, o'erwhelmed in dust obscure,
    No more, as erst, the golden goblet glows.

XV.

Sore beat by storms in Glory's arduous way,
    Here might Ambition muse a pilgrim sage ;
Here raptured see Religion's evening ray
    Gild the calm walks of his reposing age.

XVI.

Here ancient Art her Dedal fancies played
    In the quaint mazes of the crispèd roof ;
In mellow glooms the speaking pane arrayed,
    And ranged the clustered column, massy proof.

XVII.

Here Learning, guarded from a barbarous age,
    Hovered awhile, nor dared attempt the day ;
But patient, traced upon the pictured page
    The holy legend or heroic lay.

XVIII.

Hither the solitary minstrel came,
    An honoured guest ; while the grim evening sky
Hung lowering, and around the social flame
    Tuned his bold harp to deeds of chivalry.

XIX.

Thus sings the Muse, all pensive and alone,
    Nor scorns within the deep fane's inmost cell
To pluck the gray moss from the mantled stone,
    Some holy founder's mouldering name to spell.

XX.

Thus sings the Muse, yet, partial as she sings,
  With fond regret surveys these ruined piles ;
And with fair images of ancient things
  The captive bard's obsequious mind beguiles.

XXI.

But much we pardon to th' ingenuous Muse
  Her fairy shapes are tricked by fancy's pen ;
Severer reason forms far other views,
  And scans the scene with philosophic ken.

XXII.

From these deserted domes new glories rise,
  More useful institutes adorning man ;
Manners enlarged, and new civilities,
  On fresh foundations build the social plan.

XXIII.

Science, on ampler plume, a bolder flight
  Essays—escaped from Superstition's shrine ;
While freed Religion, like primæval light
  Bursting from Chaos, spreads her warmth divine.

This was written at Vale Royal. Thomas Warton, the historian of English poetry, as he was called, was born 1728, died 1790.

Legend of the Foundation of *Vale Royal* Abbey.

PART I.

I.

RINCE *Edward* sailed from *Palestine*,
  And left the Paynim's shore ;
To *Englana*'s cliffs he ploughed the brine,
  The toil of battle o'er.

II.

A truce is won at deadly cost
  By deeds of derring do,
A way midst *Holy Land* is forced
  For pilgrims to pass through.

III.

Prince *Edward*'s standard high aloft,
  The 'Golden Dragon,' waves ;
Swelled by fair winds and breezes soft,
  Or the dark storm throb braves.

IV.

At *Sicily* bad tidings wait
  Prince *Edward*'s home-filled sail ;
King *Henry*'s reign was closed by fate ;
  England's King ! *Edward !* Hail !

V.

Away ! Away ! we cannot stay,
  Homewards our course must wing ;
No loitering here.   Away ! Away !
  Fair *England* waits her King.

VI.

Again starts forth the gallant bark,
  Pressed on like fiery steed ;
In noonday bright, through midnight dark,
  Ne'er slacked its headlong speed.

VII.

The crew of home 'gan dream apart,
  Or talk of hopes and fears,
Which the long absent wanderer's heart
  So often frights and cheers.

VIII.

' There's many a slip twixt cup and lip,'
  So sages say of old ;
Before she *England* sights, the ship
  Must dangers breast untold.

IX.

A wild storm rose—against the side
  Wild winds and billows beat,
Sad are the perils ships betide
  When sky and waters meet.

X.

O'er the roused ocean broods dark night ;
  ˄ Darkness, like *Egypt*'s, dire,
Save where forked lightnings threatenings write
  In characters of fire.

XI.

Then paled the face of many a knight,
  And eke of warrior brave,
Who oft had dared grim death in fight,
  But shrank from watery grave.

XII.

In honour's cause, we thousands know
  Who 'd desperate danger face ;
Scale beetling rock—charge 'whelming foe
  To win bright valour's race.

XIII.

Patent to all their deeds appear,
  Known, how and when, they fell ;
If stretched upon a bloody bier,
  Minstrels their fame will tell.

XIV.

But thus to die !—for funeral wail
  Of friends, the howling wind !
To sink !—nor leave of death a tale,
  Not e'en a track behind !

XV.

Not gathered to that spot in death
  Where their forefathers lie !
Their shroud, the tangled sea-weed wreath ;
  The waves, their lullaby !

XVI.

Fiercer and louder howls the gale ;
  Higher, wild waters rise !
Helpless the ship, split every sail,
  The sport of ocean lies.

XVII.

King *Edward*, prostrate on his face,
  To *Mary*, heavenly maid,
Suppliant at Heaven's throne for grace,
  Thus life and mercy prayed.

KING EDWARD'S PRAYER.

Virgin Mother ! *Mary* blest !
Thou alone canst give us rest !
Curb the wild winds, smooth the wave,
None but thou our lives can save.
Home we left, to rescue land
Profaned by false prophet's band,

Where thy dear Son was born and bled,
By murderers to slaughter led.
In His name, preserve the host
Which to Holy Land hath crost.
Virgin *Mary !* hear our prayer,
Make the Red Cross knight thy care ;
Should we *England* see again
I will raise to thee a fane
Where, till time shall be no more,
Priests in chorus shall adore
Holy name of *Mary* good,
And King *Edward*'s gratitude.
Thus shall to the world proclaim
Virgin *Mary*'s blessed name
Who his help in danger came.

PART II.

I.

The mountain volume of a wave
  (Which, had it struck the bark
Had whelmed all in a common grave,
  Like Deluge—round the ark)

II.

Sank spellbound—such the force of prayer
  In peril's deadly hour :
Vain 't is for th' elements to dare
  The Virgin mother's power.

III.

The fury of the hurricane
  Stopped short in midway flight ;
The wintry chill of driving rain
  Gave way to warm sunlight.

IV.

A joyous cry of ' Land ! ' What land ?
  'T is *England*'s longed-for shore.
Spread out to view that well-loved strand
  They 'd thought to see no more !

V.

Last to fly danger, first to face,
  King *Edward* landed last ;
And thanked the Virgin's power and grace
  That fear of death was past.

VI.

The warriors throng the well-known shore,
  And disembark in haste ;
Still, still, they seem to hear the roar
  Of the stirred ocean's waste.

VII.

But when from land they seaward look,
  Amazed they gaze around ;
The vessel they had just forsook
  Had sunk in depths profound.

VIII.

So from the fight the wounded steed
    With desperate courage flies;
His rider saves in utmost need,
    Then, without struggle, dies.

IX.

The vow the king in danger made
    Was not in safety lost;
The Virgin's care was soon repaid
    To Heaven, at princely cost.

X.

With following rare, in royal state,
    He *Chester's* county sought;
Princes and nobles round him wait,
    Eke his fair queen he brought.

XI.

And at *Vale Royal* kingly hands
    Laid the foundation stone
Of abbey, which for beauty stands
    In loveliness alone.

XII.

Heaven long had marked that spot her own,
    For on the Virgin's day,
In ' *Queterne Hallowes* ' forest lone,
    Strange sights were seen, they say.

XIII.

As, when a St. *Clair*'s death throe 's near,
    In *Roslyn* chapel aisle,
Of bright unearthly lights we hear
    Amidst that fretted pile.

XIV.

So, in the stillest hours of night,
    Shepherds, awe-struck, would mark
Vale Royal woods, with splendour bright,
    Whilst all around was dark.

XV.

And angel forms, in robes of fire,
    In countless troops stood round ;
Whilst music of a heavenly choir
    Breathed forth its holy sound.

XVI.

Along the breeze soft notes would steal,
    As if from fairy land ;
And bells rang out a midnight peal
    Touched by no mortal hand !

First Part. Stanza 1. ' A truce is won ;' this was for ten years.

Stanza 4. ' At Sicily,' &c. Edward heard of the death of his son and father at Sicily on his way home. The King of Sicily remarked with surprise ' that his father's death seemed to affect him more than that of his son.' Edward replied, that ' The latter might be replaced, but that the death of a father was irreparable.'

Second Part. Stanza 12. ' Queterne Hallowes' was the old name of Vale Royal.

Stanza 14. Old tradition.

The Devil and the Monk.

A Legend of Merton Sands.

[Merton Sands were situated about a mile from Over. There used to be a festal gathering there every year for the purpose of ploughing Merton Sands, the origin of which is given below.]

I.

E barons and maidens of lofty degree,
Come list to a tale that was whispered to me ;
How once in *Vale Royal* a Friar uncivil
In knavish contrivance outwitted the Devil.

II.

The monks were asleep, and the moon it shone clear,
When the Devil came flying o'er fair *Delamere*,
And fat Friar *Francis* in dreams did assail,
With pasties of venison and flagons of ale.

III.

' Oh Friar, of ale thou shalt wassail thy fill
If I may be witness to this thy last will,
And all the fat bucks in broad *Cheshire* are thine
If here on this parchment thy name thou wilt sign.'

IV.

The scroll was unrolled, and in letters of fire
Shone forth the last will of fat *Francis* the Friar;
And thus it was worded, as I have been told
By a major acquainted with black letters old.

WILL.

I gibe and bequeath all the goods that I habe
To those who shall carry my corpse to the grabe;
And when he has done what I gibe him to do,
My soul to the undersigned witness may go.

V.

Agreed, said the Monk ; and Agreed, said the Devil ;
And each put his hand to that document evil.
Friar *Francis* his thumb on the wafer did stick,
Signed, sealed, and delivered as witness, *Old Nick.*

VI.

The papers were settled—'And now!' quoth the Friar,
'From you, Father of Evil, three things I require :
The first, good buck venison till appetite fail ;
The second, unlimited hogsheads of ale.'

VII.

'All right,' quoth the Devil ; 'but now let me hear
What's the third thing you want besides venison and beer?'
'Why this,' said the Friar, 'that on yonder sands
Of *Merton*, you twine me a dozen hay-bands.'

VIII.

The Devil sought grass by the light of the moon,
And the Devil he searched in the sunshine of noon;
And the Devil he wandered from *Mersey* to *Dee,*
But nowhere on *Merton* Sands band twisted he.

IX.

The Abbot he sat on his cushion of state,
Good ale he quaffed down and buck venison he ate;
But long as his monks in good living may revel
He never again will say 'Done' to the Devil.

X.

And whilst in fair *Cheshire* stout yeomen are found,
On those *Merton* Sands they shall fallow the ground,
Where never a blade of green grass must remain
Lest the Devil come back to *Vale Royal* again.

THE POET DRAYTON.

The Men of *Cheshire*.

[In Drayton's ' Barons' Wars,' Stanza 52, is the following notice of the men of Cheshire.]

THE noble Welsh of th' ancient British race ;
From *Lancashire* men famous for their bows ;
The men of *Cheshire* chiefest for their place,
Of bone so big as only made for blows,
And have been ever fearful to their foes.
The Northern men in feuds so deadly fell,
That for their spear and horsemanship excel.

Fearful has here a curious meaning, viz. causing fear to others.   Drayton uses *dread*
in the same sense.

Motto of *Cheshire.*

[In the 23rd Song of Drayton's 'Polyolbion' the mottoes of most of the English counties are given ; the following is that of Cheshire given by him.]

LD *Cheshire* is well-known to be the Chief of Men.

And again in Song XI.

'For which our proverb calls her *Cheshire Chief of Men.*'

Each in their order as they mustered were
Or by the difference of their colours known.

Cheshire a banner very square and broad
Wherein a man upon a lion rode.

Emblem of *Cheshire.*

[Michael Drayton, a poet, was born about 1563. He wrote a poem on the battle of Agincourt, and describes the men of the different county regiments embarking :—
    ' Each in their order as they mustered were
    Or by the difference of their armings known
    Or by their colours.'
After mentioning the distinctive emblems of many counties, the following stanza occurs in which the emblem of Cheshire is given as i was at the beginning of the fifteenth century.]

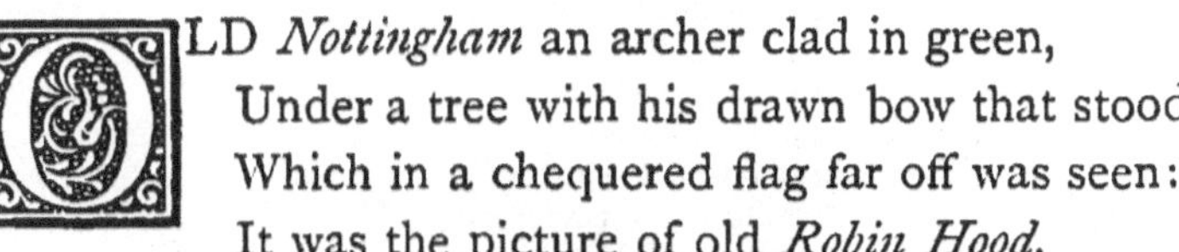

OLD *Nottingham* an archer clad in green,
    Under a tree with his drawn bow that stood,
    Which in a chequered flag far off was seen:
    It was the picture of old *Robin Hood.*
And *Lancashire,* not as the least I ween,
Thro' three crowns three arrows smeared with blood.
Cheshire, a banner very square and broad,
Whereon a man upon a lion rode.

Polyolbion.

[Drayton wrote a topographical poem, called 'Polyolbion,' in thirty books or songs, the first eighteen of which he published in 1612. The eleventh song treats chiefly of Cheshire, and has been frequently quoted; what refers to the County Palatine in that song is as follows:

> The muse, her native earth to see,
> Returns to England over Dee ;
> Visits stout Cheshire, and there shews
> To her and hers what Cheshire owes.
> And of the nymphlets sporting there,
> In Wyrral and in Delamere,
> Weever the great devotion sings,
> Of the religious Saxon kings.
> Those riverets doth together call,
> Which into him and Mersey fall.
> &c.   &c.   &c.]

WITH as unwearied wings, and in as high a gait,
As when we first set forth observing every state,
The muse from *Cambria* comes with pinions summ'd
And having put herself upon the English ground, [and sound;
First seizeth in her course the noblest *Cestrian* shore
Of our great English bloods, as careful here of yore
As *Cambria* of her brutes now is or could be then,
For which our proverb calls her ' *Cheshire* Chief of Men.'
And of our counties place of Palatine doth hold,
And thereto hath her high legalities enrolled.
Besides, in many fields since conquering *William* came,
Her people she hath proved, to her eternal fame :

All children of her own, the leader and the led,
The mightiest men of bone in her full bosom bred ;
And neither of them such as cold penurious need
Spurs to each rash attempt ; but such as soundly feed,
Clad in warm English cloth ; and maimed should they return
(Whom this false ruthless world else from their doors would
Have livelihood of their own their ages to sustain.   [spurn)
Nor did the tenant's pay the landlord's charge maintain,
But as abroad in war he spent of his estate,
Returning to his home, his hospitable gate
The richer and the poor stood open to receive.
They of all *England* most to ancient customs cleave,
Their yeomanry, and still endeavour to uphold ;
For rightly whilst herself brave *England* was of old,
And our courageous kings us forth to conquest led,
Our armies in those times (near through the world so dread)
Of our tall yeomen were, and footmen for the most,
Who (with their bills and bows) can confidently boast,
Our leopards they so long and bravely did advance
Above the fleur-de-lys, even in the heart of *France.*
O thou thrice happy shire confined so to be
'Twixt two so famous floods as *Mersey* is and *Dee !*
Thy *Dee* upon the west from *Wales* doth thee divide,
Thy *Mersey* on the north from the Lancastrian side,
Thy natural sister shire, and linkt unto thee so
That *Lancashire* along with *Cheshire* still doth go.
As towards the Derbian *Peak* and *Moreland* (which do draw
More mountainous and wild), the high-crowned *Shutlingslaw*
And *Molcop* be thy mounds, with those proud hills whence rove
The lovely sister brooks, the silvery *Dane* and *Dove*—

Clear *Dove* that makes to *Trent*, the other to the west ;
But in that famous town most happy of the rest
(From which thou takest thy name), fair *Chester*, called of old
Carlegion, whilst proud *Rome* her conquests here did hold;
Of those her legions known the faithful station then,
So stoutly held to tack by those near North *Wales* men ;
Yet by her own right name had rather called be,
As her the Britons termed the fortress upon *Dee*.
Than vainly she would seem a miracle to stand
Th' imaginary work of some huge giant's hand,
Which, if such ever where, tradition tells not who—
But back awhile my muse to *Weever* let us go,
Which (with himself compared) each British flood doth scorn ;
His fountain and his fall, both *Chester*'s rightly born.
The country in his course that clean he doth divide,
Cut in two equal shares upon his either side.
And what that famous flood far more than all enriches
The bracky fountains are those two renowned *Wyches !*
The *Nant-Wych* and the *North*—whose either briny well
For store and sorts of salts make *Weever* to excel.
Besides their general use, not had by him in vain,
But in himself thereby doth holiness retain
Above his fellow floods, whose healthful virtues taught
Hath of the sea gods oft caused *Weever* to be sought
For physick in their need; and *Thetis* oft hath seen,
When by their wanton sports her *Nerides* have been,
So sick that *Glaucus'* self hath failed in their cure,
Yet *Weever* by his salts recovery durst assure.
And *Amphitrite* oft this wizard river led
Into her secret walks (the depths profound and dread)

Of him (supposed so wise), the hid events to know
Of things that were to come, as things done long ago—
In which he had been proved most exquisite to be ;
And bare his fame so far that oft twixt him and *Dee*
Much strife there hath arose in their prophetic skill.
But to conclude our praise—our *Weever* here doth will
The muse his source to sing, as how his course he steers,
Who from his natural spring, as from the neighbouring meres,
Sufficiently supplied shoots forth his silver breast,
As though he meant to take directly towards the east,
Until at length he proves he loitereth but to play
Till *Ashbrook* and the *Lee* o'ertake him on his way.
Which to his journey's end him earnestly do haste
Till, having got to *Wych*, he taketh there a taste
Of her most savoury salt, is by the sacred touch
Forced faster in his course, his motion quickened much,
To *Northwych*, and at last as he approacheth near
Dane, *Whelock* draws then *Crock* from the black ominous mere,
Accounted one of those that *England*'s wonders make ;
Of neighbours *Blackmere* named, of strangers *Brereton's Lake*.
Whose property seems far from reasons why to stand :
For near before his death that's owner of the land
She sends up stocks of trees that on the top do float,
By which the world her first did for a wonder note.
His handmaid *Howty* next to *Weever* holds her race,
When *Peever*, with the help of *Pickmere*, makes apace
To put in with those streams his sacred steps that tread
Into the mighty waste of *Mersey* him to lead ;
Where, when the rivers meet with all their stately train,
Proud *Mersey* is so great of entering the main,

As he would make a show for empery to stand,
And wrest the threeforkt mace from out stern *Neptune*'s hand.
To *Cheshire* highly bound for that his wat'ry store,
As to the grosser locks on the Lancastrian shore.
From hence he getteth *Goyt* down from his Peakish spring,
And *Bollin* that along doth nimbler *Birken* bring
From *Maxfield*'s mighty wilds, of whose shaggy Silvans she
Hath in the rocks been wooed, her paramour to be ;
Who in the darksome holes and caverns kept her long,
And that proud forest made a party to her wrong :
Yet could not all entreat the pretty brook to stay
Which to her stream sweet *Bollin* creeps away ;
To whom upon her road she pleasantly reports
The many mirthful jests and wanton woodish sports
In *Maxfield* they have had, as of that forest's fate,
Until they come at length where *Mersey* for more state,
Assuming broader banks himself, so proudly bears,
That at his stern approach extended *Wirral* fears
That what betwixt his floods of *Mersey* and the *Dee*,
In very little time devoured he might be.
Out of the foaming surge till *Hilbre* lifts his head
To let the foreland see how richly he had sped.
    &c. &c.

What follows does not refer to Cheshire.

Belfry Rhymes.

[Formerly existing at Holmes Chapel.]

WHOEVER rings with spur or hat
    Shall pay the clerk a groat for that ;
    Whoever swears, or bell turns o'er,
    Shall forfeit fourpence, if not more ;
If any shall do aught amiss
Threepence the forfeit is.
Observe these laws, and break them not,
Lest you lose your pence for that.

A Legend of *Combermere*.

I.

HE sun shone clear on the broad bright mere,
   And the menials thronged its shore :
They sought to guide from the deep flood tide
   The bells of the monks of yore.

II.

When lo, from the mere, these words of fear
   Struck awe to the listeners round ;
It seemed from the wave some spirit gave
   That supernatural sound.

III.

' Let none who would sweep these bells from the deep
   One word unholy use ;
Or his strength shall be vain, and never again
   Shall they rise from their watery ooze.

IV.

And deep mid the wave shall be his grave,
   An undiscovered tomb ;
And this smiling shore shall smile no more
   Till the fated blast of doom.'

V.

With awe and fear the menials steer
   A vast bell to the side,
Till it rests on land, and with eager hand
   One grasped its rim and cried—

VI.

'Though earth and air and the waters there,
   Conspire with the massive bell;
In spite of them all, it no more shall fall,
   I swear by the fiends of hell!'

VII.

Scarce had he spoke when with thundering stroke
   The crumbling earth gave way,
And the waters swell o'er the holy bell
   And the sinful son of clay.

VIII.

They dragged the mere both far and near,
   But their comrade never found;
And their sons still tell of the holy bell
   That the impious scorner drowned.

The bells of Combermere Abbey are said to have been removed to Wrenbury Church, and to be identical with those still there.

Barning the *Appleton* Thorn.

[This merrymaking (now discontinued) used to be held annually on the 29th of June,
St. Peter's day. The adjoining public-house is the Thorn. R. E. Warburton (the lord of
the manor) some years since replaced the old dead thorn.]

CHORUS.

ARN the old Thorn
 At peep of dawn,
 This happy morn
  Barn the Thorn.

I.

Hasten lads and lassies all,
Here together neighbours call ;
Let the trumpet's brazen tongue
Summons all, both old and young.

     Chorus, Barn &c.

II.

Years, years ago thy shade hath seen
Our grandames dancing on the green,
Hath seen our sires as wee things play
And while the summer hours away.

     Chorus, Barn &c.

III.

Branches of thy fragrant May,
By love-sick swain, at break of day
Have oft been hung at maiden's door,
With Nature's gems bespangled o'er.
Chorus, Barn &c.

IV.

Here vows of love have oft been made
By fond youth whispering in thy shade ;
Oft hath the evening breeze I wiss
Mixed with the murmur of a kiss.
Chorus, Barn &c.

V.

Thy ruby stores (to childhood's eye
So beautiful), when winter 's nigh,
Tempt startled field-fares to thy tree,
By hunger tamed, to feast on thee.
Chorus, Barn &c.

VI.

Slowly beneath thy boughs hath past,
When earth to earth returns at last
As generations melt away,
The weeping funeral array.
Chorus, Barn &c.

VII.

But to-day away with sorrow,
Nought shall grieve us till to-morrow :
With dance and feast and village lay
We'll celebrate our barning day.
Chorus, Barn &c.

VIII.

Clip the hawthorn, scatter flowers,
Rob for this the brightest bowers ;
Urge on the dance and wassail—say
We will, we will be mad to-day.

CHORUS.

Barn the old Thorn
At peep of dawn,
This happy morn
Barn the Thorn.

' Barn the Thorn.' Wilbraham, in his Glossary, calls it bawming (which means the same thing). Mr. Beamont, our accurate local antiquary, tells me the inhabitants of Appleton called it 'barning,' i.e. adorning.

Stanza 3. ' Branches of thy fragrant May,' &c. Hanging up a branch of May-flowers at your sweetheart's door was considered most complimentary ; but if a maiden in Cheshire finds an ouler branch (alder) hung up at her door, she knows some one considers her a scold.

Inscription for the Ale House (near *Appleton* Thorn) called the ' Thorn.'

AS long as you 're sober you 're safe at the *Thorn*,
But if drunk over night it will prick you next morn ;
May the lord of the manor who planted it thrive,
May the wenches who bawm it all speedily wive ;
May the old 'neath its shadow in comfort repose,
And *Appleton* flourish as long as it grows.

A Song for the *Teucerean* Archers of Stockport.

I.

HOW happy are archers who draw the long bow,
No pastime affords such diversion below,
The hours of our sport seem to pass on by stealth
In manly exertion conducive to health ;
Like *Sherwood* free rangers our skill we display,
With harmony closing the sport of the day.

II.

Whenever bold *Robin* his bugle-horn blew,
Their bows they unstrung, and relaxed the stiff yew ;
Then sung the achievements of archers so good,
Whilst 'Hey down a down' echoed through the greenwood.
Like them, ere the dew fall, our bows we unstring,
And songs to the honour of archery sing.

III.

No sports of the field can with archery vie.
Let hunters dash after the hounds at full cry,
Our archery well every muscle can brace,
And we run no risks like the sons of the chase;
While at this diversion our skill we display,
With harmony closing the sport of the day.

IV.

What toils on the heath, all bespattered and wet,
A sportsman must take if some grouse he would get :
In cold, hail, and rain he the weather must stand,
While we have refreshment and shelter at hand ;
Where if the sky lowers we partake of good cheer,
And again bend our bows when the weather is clear.

V.

With dog and with gun who would now range the fields ;
Laborious the toil, and small purchase it yields :
But archers, whene'er to the ground they resort,
Defy any poachers for spoiling their sport ;
While at their diversion their skill they display,
With harmony closing the sport of the day.

VI.

Then here 's to all archers—long may they survive,
And still at their art for the mastery strive,

When, aged, no more their long bows can they bend,
With health, independence, a bottle and friend ;
Respected by archers, free, social, and gay,
May they talk of the matches they shot in their day.

This song must have been written towards the end of the eighteenth century.

[In a song composed upon archery, by Ogden, in the general enumeration of the different archery clubs at that time existing in different counties of England, is the following notice of the Teucerean Archers, for whom the preceding song was written by Travis.]

TEUCEREAN archers in the art are skilled :
    Part make their arrows fit for every length,
    And finished well in feather, notch, and pile.
    These meet where *Stockport* rears her hilly streets,
High towering o'er the rocky banks of *Tame*,
And holds a charter from her ancient lord,
Who granted every burgess of his land
An acre, with a homestead for a house,
On payment each of twelve pence yearly rent.
Sure money then was scarce, or lords were good ;
'T is plenty now, or rents too high are raised.'

In an earlier part of the same poem is the following :—

Again, on *Crispin*'s day at *Agincourt*
The English bowmen triumphed part in front,
Led by the King, of *Cheshire* men the chief.

And again, further on :—

> A greater slaughter yet at *Flodden Field*
> Took place where *Scotland*'s king in person fought,
> And fighting, fell ; Lancastrian bowmen there
> Were much distinguished, *Stanley* led them on.
> With these the *Cheshire* men from *Mersey*'s banks,
> And sedgy *Weever* to the rapid *Dee*.
>
> &c.   &c.

A Bowmeeting Song.

Sung at the Meeting of Cheshire Archers at Arley Hall, 1851.

I.

THE tent is pitched, the target reared, the ground is
    measured out,
  For the weak arm sixty paces, and one hundred for
    the stout ;
Come gather ye together then, the youthful and the fair,
And poet's lay to distant day the victor shall declare.

II.

Let busy fingers lay aside the needle and the thread,
To prick the golden canvas with a pointed arrow head ;
Ye sportsmen quit the stubble, ye fishermen the stream,
Fame and glory stand before you, brilliant eyes around you
  beam.

III.

All honour to the long bow, which many a battle won
Ere powder blazed or bullet flew from arquebus or gun ;
All honour to the long bow, which merry men of yore
With hound and horn at early morn in greenwood forest bore.

IV.

Oh famous is the archer's sport, 't was honoured long ago ;
The God of Love, the God of Wit, bore both of them a bow ;
Love laughs to-day in beauty's eye and blushes in her cheek,
And wit is heard in every word that merry archers speak.

V.

The archer's heart, though like his bow a tough and sturdy thing,
Is pliant still and yielding when affection pulls the string ;
All his words and all his actions are like arrows pointed well
To hit that golden centre where true love and friendship dwell.

VI.

They tell us in that outline which the lips of beauty show
How *Cupid* found a model for his heart-subduing bow,
The arrows in his quiver are the glances from her eye,
A feather from Love's wing it is that makes the arrow fly.

Belfry Rhymes.

St. John's Church, Chester.   Date 1627.

YOU ringers all observe these orders well,
    he forfits 12 pence who turns ore a bell ;
    & he y^t ringes with either spurr or hatt
    his 6 pence certainely shall pay for y^t,
& he that spoile or doth disturbe a peale
shall pay his 4 pence or a cann of ale,
and he that is harde to curse or sweare
shall pay his 12 pence, and forbeare.
These customes elsewhere now are used
lest bells and ringers be abused.
you gallants then y^t on purpose come to ring
see that you coyne alonge with you dothe bringe ;
and further also, if y^t you ring here,
you must ring truly with hande and eare,
or else your forfits surely pay
full speedily, and that without delay ;
our laws are old, y^y are not new,
The sextone looketh for his due.

ANAGRAM ON RANDLE HOLMES.

Lo Men's Herald.

NIXON, THE CHESHIRE PROPHET.

Nixon, the *Palatine* Prophet.

> ' Thou Palatine Prophet, whose fame I revere,
> Woe be to that bard who speaks ill of a seer.'

So sings Warburton.   In a book professing to be a collection of the legends and old lore of Cheshire we could not omit all mention of Nixon, yet what are we to say of our county Nostradamus?   One account affirms that he was born in the time of Edward IV., about 1467.   One of the prophecies, or rather an act of second sight (as they call it in the Highlands) attributed to him, was (whilst ploughing in Cheshire) speaking of the battle of Bosworth, and the result of the battle, which was being fought at that very time in Leicestershire (August 22, 1485, a curious time for ploughing).   Miss Wilbraham utilises the idea of his having been born in the reign of Edward IV. in ' For and Against,' her accurate tale of the fifteenth century.   It is, however, a curious thing that the first printed account of Nixon is that of ' Oldmixon,' published in 1714, which opens thus :—

> ' In the reign of James I. there lived a fool whose name was Nixon.'

Here is at once a discrepancy of some 150 years in the date of the two accounts of his birth.   The more the accounts of Nixon have been ventilated by our Cheshire historians, the more problematical and irreconcilable they are.   He is said to have been born at Over, and though his reputed residence (Bridge-end House) is pointed out, no mention is made of him in the registers of Over or Whitegate ; and the very existence of the house in which he was born would at any rate disprove his birth in 1467.   He is said to have been starved to death at Hampton Court by the negligence of the servants, who had (during the temporary absence of the Court) shut him up for some peccadillo, and forgotten him.   A closet at that palace, pointed out now as the scene of his death, was built in the reign of William III., and the whole palace was built subsequently to the reign of Henry VII., during which period, according to some accounts, Nixon died.   The particulars relating to the Cholmondeley family of Vale Royal, mentioned in the printed accounts of Nixon's life, do not tally with the known history of that family.   No author I understand who might have been contemporary with Nixon in either the reigns of Edward IV. or James I. mentions him, and the first printed account of him, as I said before, did not appear till ninety years after the death of James I.   In the ' Iter Lancastriense,' written by Richard James in 1636, is a trace, and a doubtful trace, of one of the prophecies attributed to Nixon, in one of the later published accounts of his life :—

> ' Whose safetye gave occasion to ould laws
> Thus riming—" When all England is alofte,
> Then happie they whose dwellings in God's crofte."
> And where thinke you this crofte of Christe should be
> But midst Ribchester's Ribble and the Dee.'

In Nixon's life we have the following. One asked Nixon 'Where he might be safe in those days?'—he answered,

> 'In God's croft, betwixt the rivers Mersey and Dee.'

But other counties seem also to have their preordained sanctuary. In Yorkshire we find the following version :—

> 'When all the world shall be aloft
> Then Hallamshire shall be God's croft.'

Many ingenious completions of Nixon's prophecies have been given to the world, but it is wonderful how we find a clever person work out the accomplishment of a prophecy he is predetermined to prove.

Amongst Nixon's prophecies is the following:

> 'Then rise up Richard, son of Richard,
> And bless the happy reign,' &c. &c.

No *Richard* came, so it was changed to *George*, the son of *George*.

One of the ingenious readings of prophecy (not one of Nixon's) is the following. There was an old saying, whence originating is not very clear,

> When *Hempe* is spun
> *England*'s done.

The initials of Henry VIII.
> Edward VI.
> Mary
> and
> Philip,
> Elizabeth,

spell Hempe. At Elizabeth's death ' England was done,' being united to Scotland by Elizabeth's successor, James I., and becoming Great Britain.

The conclusion I should come to with respect to our ' Palatine Prophet' is this. That a man called Nixon (which was probably a soubriquet and not the original name, which will account for not finding the name in the registers) existed at Over. He was probably called by the ignorant peasants (with whom *omne ignotum* is *pro magnifico*) Nick's son, or the son of the Devil, from the supernatural knowledge they attributed to him, and which the vulgar of all ages are more apt to consider as originating in Hell than in Heaven. When Nixon lived is a myth. He was probably a half-witted clown, or not ' all there,' as we say in Cheshire, but gifted with considerable shrewdness and cunning (not incompatible with a partially diseased brain); and that, like the pretenders to second sight in Scotland, he may have occasionally made some happy guesses, and may have become acquainted with facts and realities during the rambling life so frequently preferred by those who are not quite right in their upper stories, the retailing of which among the stay-at-home rustics of his own neighbourhood invested everything he said with a sort of mystic authority and credit. During his time, and since he has passed away, the prophetical allusions and dark sayings of the county, however and from whomsoever originating, have been attributed to Nixon; just as in Sheridan's time all the sharp sayings of the period were fathered on him. The first editions of ' Nixon's Life ' contain very few prophecies in comparison with the later editions. The following is from an old edition, where we find more than double the prophecies of the original (1714 A.D.) edition :—

The Original Predictions of *Robert Nixon*.

HEN a Raven shall build in a stone Lion's mouth,
    On a church top beside the grey forest,
Then shall a King of *England* be drove from his
    crown,
    And return no more.

When an Eagle shall sit on the top of *Vale Royal* House,
Then shall an heir be born who shall live to see great troubles
    in *England*.

    There shall be a Miller named *Peter*,
        With two heels on one foot,
    Who shall distinguish himself bravely,
        And shall be knighted by the victor ;
    For foreign nations shall invade *England*,
        But the invader shall be killed,
    And laid across a horse's back,
        And led in triumph.

A Boy shall be born with three thumbs on one hand,
  Who shall hold three Kings' horses,
Whilst *England* three times is won and lost in one day.
  But after this shall be happy days,
  A new set of people of virtuous manners
    Shall live in peace.
But the wall of *Vale Royal* near the pond shall be the token of
  its truth,
For it shall fall.
  If it fall downwards,
Then shall the church be sunk for ever ;
But if it fall upwards against a hill,
Then shall the church and honest men live still.
Under this wall shall be found the bones of a British King ;
Peckforton Mill shall be removed to *Luddington Hill*,
And three days' blood shall turn *Noginshire* Mill.

    But beware of a chance to the Lord of *Oulton*,
    Lest he should be hanged at his own door.

    A Crow shall sit on the top of Headless Cross
      In the forest so grey,
    And drink of the nobles' gentle blood so free.
    Twenty thousand horses shall want masters
    Till their girths rot under their bellies.

    Through our own money and our own men
    Shall a dreadful war begin.
    Between the sickle and the suck
    All *England* shall have a pluck,
    And be several times forsworn,

> And put to their wits' end,
> That it shall not be known
> Whether to reap their corn,
> Bury their dead,
> Or go to the field to fight.
> A great scarcity of bread corn.

Foreign nations shall invade *England* with snow on their helmets,
And shall bring plague, famine, and murder in the skirts of their
  garments.

> A great tax shall be granted but never gathered.
> Between a rick and two trees
> A famous battle fought shall be.
> *London* Street shall run with blood,
> And at last shall sink.
> So that it shall be fulfilled,
> *Lincoln* was, *London* is, and *York* shall be
> The finest city of the three.

There will be three gates in *London*, of imprisoned men for
  cowsters ;
Then if you have three cows, at the first gate sell one and keep
  thee at home,
At the second gate sell the other two, and keep thee at home,
At the last gate all shall be done
When summer in winter shall come,
And peace is made at every man's home.
Then shall be danger of war,
For though with peace at night shall nations ring,
Men shall rise to war in the morning.

There will be a winter council, a careful Christmas, and
    bloody Lent.
In those days there shall be hatred and bloodshed :
The father against the son, the son against the father,
That one may have a house for lifting the latch of the door.
Landlords shall stand with hat in their hands
To desire their tenants to hold their lands.

    Great wars and pressing of soldiers,
    But at last clubs and clouted shoes shall carry the day.

It will be good in those days for a man to sell his goods and
    keep close at home.
      Then forty pounds in hand
      Will be better than forty pounds a year in land.
      The Cock of the North will be made to flee,
      And his feathers be plucked for his pride,
      That he shall almost curse the day he was born.
One asked *Nixon* where he might be safe in those days?
           He answered
    In *God*'s croft between the rivers *Mersey* and *Dee*.

    Scotland shall stand more or less
    Till it has brought *England* to a piteous case.
    The *Scots* shall rule *England* one whole year.

Three years of great wars,
And in all countries great uproars :
The first is terrible, the second worse, but the third unbearable!

Three great Battles :
   One at *Northumberland Bridge,*
   One at *Cumberland Bridge,*
   And the other the South side of the *Trent.*

Crows shall drink the blood of many nobles,
East shall rise against West, and North against South.

   Then take this for good :
   Noginshire Mill shall run with blood,
   And many shall fly down *Wanslow Lane.*

A man shall come into *England,*
But the Son of a King crowned with Thorns
Shall take from him the Victory.
Many Nobles shall fight,
But a Bastard Duke shall win the day;
And so without delay
Set *England* in a right way.
A Wolf from the East shall right eagerly come
On the South side of *Sandford* on a grey *Monday* morning,
  Where groves shall grow upon a green.
Beside green, grey, they shall flee
  Into rocks, and many die.
They shall flee into *Salt Strand,*
And twenty thousand without sword shall die each man.

  The dark Dragon over *Sudsbrown*
    Shall bring with him a royal Band,
    But their lives shall be forlorn ;
  His head shall be in *Stafford* town,
    His tail in *Ireland.*

He boldly shall bring his men, thinking to win renown,
Beside a wall in forest fair he shall be beaten down.

On *Hines Heath* they shall begin the bloody fight,
And with trained steed shall hew each other's helmet bright ;
But who shall win that day no one can tell.

A Duke out of *Denmark* shall him dight
On a day in *England*, and make many a Lord full low to light,
And the Ladies cry well away !
And the black fleet with main and might
Their enemies full boldly there assail.
In *Britain*'s land shall be a Knight
On them shall make a cruel fight ;
A bitter Boar with main and might
Shall bring a royal rout that day.
There shall die many a worthy knight,
And be driven into the fields green and grey ;
They shall lose both field and fight.

The weary Eagle shall to an island in the sea retire,
Where leaves and herbs grow fresh and green,
There shall he meet a ladye fair,
Who shall say, ' Go help thy friend in battle slain :'
Then by the counsel of that fair
He eagerly will make to flee
Twenty-six standard of the enemy.
A rampant Lion in silver set in armour fair
Shall help the eagle in that tide,
When many a knight shall die.

The **Bear** that hath been long tied to a stake shall shake his
    chains,
That every man shall hear, and shall cause much debate.
The Bull and the Red Rose shall stand in strife,
That shall turn *England* to much woe,
And cause many a man to lose his life.

In a forest stand oaks three,
    Beside a headless cross ;
A well of blood shall run and ree,
    Its cover shall be Brass,
      Which shall never appear
    Till Horses' feet have trod it bare.
    Who wins it will declare
    The eagle shall so fight that day,
    That ne'er a friend 's from him away.
A Hound without delay shall run the chace far and near.
    The dark Dragon shall die in fight,
A lofty head the Bear shall rear,
    The wide Wolf so shall light
The bridled steed against his enemies will fiercely fight.

    A fleet shall come out of the North,
      Riding on a horse of trees ;
    A white hind beareth he,
    And the wreaths so free.

That day the Eagle shall him slay,
    And in a hill set his banner straightway,
That Lion who 's forsaken been and forced to flee,
    Shall hear a woman shrilly say,
' Thy friends are killed on yonder hill,
    Death to many a knight this day.'

With that the Lion bears his banner to a hill
   Within a forest that's so plain,
   Beside a headless cross of stone.
There shall the Eagle die that day,
   And the red Lion get renown.

A great Battle shall be fought by crowned Kings three :
One shall die, and a Bastard Duke shall win the day.
In *Sandyford* there lies a stone
A crowned King shall lose his head on.

In those wretched days five wicked priests' heads shall be sold
   for a penny.
Slaughter shall rage to such a degree,
  And infants left by those who are slain,
That damsels shall with fear and glee
  Cry, 'Mother ! Mother, here's a man !'

   Between seven, eight, and nine
   In *England* wonders shall be seen ;
   Between nine and thirteen all sorrow shall be done.

   Then rise up, *Richard* son of *Richard*,
     And bless the happy reign ;
   Thrice happy he who sees this time to come,
    When *England* shall know rest and peace again.

Nixon is also said to have predicted that Northwich should be destroyed by water.

The following is said to have been his prophecy relating to the Reformation:—

> A time shall come when Priests and Monks
> Shall have no churches nor houses,
> And places where images stood
> Lined letters shall be good ;
> English books through churches are spread,
> There shall be no holy bread.

I will only add two more of his prophecies :—

> When you the *Harrow* come on high,
> Soon a Raven's nest shall be.

> Through *Weaver* Hall shall be a lone (*i.e.* lane),
> *Ridley* Pool shall be sown and mown,
> And *Darnel* Park shall be hacked and hewn.

Among the lower orders in Cheshire there is a strong belief and faith in Nixon, and there is no story about him too wild to be believed. A man told me that Lord Delamere had cut down and sold to a carpenter the oak under which Nixon used to prophesy ; that the carpenter had made a table of part of it ; and that the vein of the wood repeated over its whole surface likenesses of Nixon ; and that Lord Delamere bought the table, which is now at Vale Royal. The only thing that spoils the interest of this tale is that it is simply false in every particular and never did occur.

Le Gros-Veneur.

Sung at the Tarporley Hunt Meeting, November 1858.

I.

MIGHTY great Hunter in deed and in name,
To our Shire long ago with the Conqueror came ;
A hunting he went with his bugle and bow,
And he shouted in *Normandy-French* ' Tallyho.'
Chorus.
The man we now place at the head of our chase
Can his pedigree trace from the Gros-Veneur !

II.

'T is a maxim by fox-hunters well understood,
That in horses and hounds there is nothing like blood;
So the chief who the fame of our kennel maintains
Should likewise be born with good blood in his veins.
Chorus.
The man we now place at the head of our chase
Can his pedigree trace from the Gros-Veneur!

III.

Old and young with delight shall the Gros-Veneur greet,
The field once again in good fellowship meet ;
The Shire with one voice shall re-echo our choice,
And again the old pastime all *Cheshire* rejoice.
Chorus.

> May the sport we ensure many seasons endure,
> And the Chief of our chase be the Gros-Veneur.

IV.

Though no more, as of yore, a long bow at his back,
Now a Gros-Veneur guides us and governs our pack ;
Again let each earth-stopper rise from his bed,
This year they shall be all well fee'd and well fed.
Chorus.

> May the sport we ensure many seasons endure,
> And the Chief of our chase be the Gros-Veneur.

V.

Let *Geoffrey* with smiles and with shillings restore
Good humour, when housewives their poultry deplore,
Well pleased for each goose on which *Reynard* had preyed
To find in their pockets a golden egg laid.
Chorus.

> May the sport we ensure many seasons endure,
> And the Chief of our chase be the Gros-Veneur.

VI.

Should our Chief with the toil of the Senate grow pale,
The elixir of life is a ride o'er the Vale;
There of health, says the Song, he shall gain a new stock,
Till the pulse beats the seconds as true as a clock.
Chorus.

> May the sport we ensure many seasons endure,
> And the Chief of our chase be the Gros-Veneur.

VII.

I defy *Normandy* now to send a Chasseur
Who can ride alongside of our Gros-Veneur;
And couching my lance, I will challenge all *France*
To outvie the bright eye of Lady *Constance.*
Chorus.

> Long, long, may she grace with her presence our chase,
> The Bride and the Pride of the Gros-Veneur.

The Battle of *Blore Heath*.

September 23, 1458.

THE 'Battle of *Blore Heath*' the place doth next supply,
Betwixt *Richard Nevil* that great Earl of *Salisbury*,
Who, with the Duke of *York*, had at *St. Albans* late
That glorious battle got with uncontrolled fate.
And *James* Lord *Audley* stirred by that revengeful Queen
To stop him on his way, for his inveterate spleen
She bare him, for that still he with the Yorkists held,
Who coming from the North (by sundry wrongs compelled
To parley with the King), the Queen that time who lay
In *Staffordshire*, and thought to stop him on his way.
That valiant *Tucket* stirred, in *Cheshire* powerful then,
T' affront him in the field, where *Cheshire* gentlemen
Divided were; one part made valiant *Tucket* strong,
The other with the Earl rose as he came along.
Encamping both their powers divided by a brook,
Whereby the prudent Earl this strong advantage took;
For putting in the field his army in array,
Then making as with speed he meant to march away,
He caused a flight of shafts to be discharged first.
The enemy, who thought that he had done his worst,

And cowardly had fled in a disordered rout,
Attempt to wade the brook, he wheeling (soon) about
Let fiercely on that part which then were passed over :
Their friends then in the rear not able to recover
The other rising bank, to lend the vanguard aid.
The Earl, who found the plot take right that he had laid,
On those that forward prest, as those that did recoil,
As hungry in Revenge there made a ravenous spoil.
There *Dutton Dutton* kills, a *Done* doth kill a *Done*,
A *Booth* a *Booth*, and *Leigh* by *Leigh* is overthrown ;
A *Venables* against a *Venables* doth stand,
A *Troutbeck* fighteth with a *Troutbeck* hand to hand ;
There *Molineux* doth make a *Molineux* to die,
And *Egerton* the strength of *Egerton* doth try.
Oh *Cheshire*, wert thou mad? of thine own native gore
So much until this day thou never shed'st before ;
Above two thousand men upon the earth were thrown,
Of which the greatest part were naturally thy own.

There is a legend that for several days before the battle of Blore Heath, there arose each morning out of the foss three mermaids, who announced the coming event by singing these lines as they combed their long tresses :—

' Ere yet the hawberry assumes its deep red
Embrued shall this heath be with blood nobly shed.'

From the Battle of Blore Heath by Mr. Beamont.
Chester Society Journal, part ii. p. 99.

LEGEND OF OVER CHURCH.

Legend of *Over* Church.

I.

NFOLD the reason, why, I pray,
Doth *Over* church from *Over* town
Stand distant many roods away ?

II.

Over church in days of yore,
So speaks traditionary lore,
Amidward *Over* stood ;

III.

There every sabbath, and each day
Marked out as Fast and Holiday,
All sought for heavenly food.

IV.

In vain the *Devil* spread his net,
The church protecting, ever let
His schemes against men's souls.

V.

Long he revolved in his black heart,
And plotted each infernal art,
        Defrauded of his tolls.

VI.

At length he rushed the church to seize,
Nor less his devilish spite might please,
        And bear it far away.

VII.

With claws the fane from earth he tore,
And on his impious wings upbore,
        One morn at break of day.

VIII.

And as his sacrilegious flight
He onward winged with demon might,
        Screamed a triumphant yell.

IX.

He dreamt not he was heard and spied
By monks he had so oft defied,
        Since first from heaven he fell.

X.

At once in holy chorus swell
Their earnest prayers (of sin the knell),
        To stay the robber's flight.

XI.

Anathemas from earth arise,
And maranathas pierce the skies
To scare the foul fiend from his prize.
          May God defend the right !

XII.

Still, undismayed, he onward flew ;
Though heavier still his burden grew,
          He held on like despair.

XIII.

What sound is that now moves fresh fears ?
The *Devil* trembles as he hears
          Bells rolling through the air.

XIV.

Hark ! from some distant tower unseen,
(*Vale Royal*'s abbey church, I ween)
          A crashing peal rings forth.

XV.

Well know we evil spirits fear
The sound of bells, so strong, so clear ;
          Such holy notes they dread.

XVI.

And oft, 'tis said, the passing bell
Scares far away the imps of *Hell*
          From dying Christian's bed.

XVII.

As *Satan* struggled on in pain,
His boasted strength begins to wane,
   Though eke by malice fed.

XVIII

Stunned by monks' prayers and pealing noise,
In vain he strives the weight to poise :
   Swift from his grasp it fell.

XIX.

He spurned the church as down it flew,
But a dark mist its mantle threw
   For safety round the pile.

XX.

Screeching with hate, mad with despair,
The fiend escaped through murky air.
   All baffled was his wile.

XXI.

The church through space descending rushed :
By its own weight it must be crushed
   Whene'er it earth may gain.

XXII.

Prostrate the monks and abbot kneel :
In *Heaven* alone aught hope they feel,
   For mortal help is vain.

XXIII.

They raised to great St. *Chad* a prayer
From bale the toppling church to spare,
    And save the perilled fane.

XXIV.

See ! as they pray, the mass floats down,
Light as the breeze borne thistle-down,
    Soft as on fleece the snow.

XXV.

Preserved it stood—there still it stands—
Rescued from sacrilegious hands,
    Escaped the foul fiend's blow.

XXVI.

Beyond ' *Town Fields* ' in valley low,
Where worshippers from *Over* go,
    And humbly offer prayers.

XXVII.

One measured mile from the old site
Where first from air it did alight,
    The church still *Satan* scares.

XXVIII.

This is the reason why they say
That *Over* church from *Over* town
Stands distant many roods away.

The Rev. C. Jackson, curate of Over, tells me that a former rector of Over (the Rev. J. Crane), when Roger Young was his curate, and Isaac Woolf was his clerk, wrote the following lines on Over church :—

> In a pleasant low vale Over church you remark
> As through Swanlow you journey along,
> Where a Crane is the vicar, a Woolf is the clerk,
> And the curate will always be Young.

There is a legend in Ireland that a fissure in a range of hills near Tipperary was caused by the Devil (enraged at St. Patrick meeting him as he was carrying some souls off to hell, and obliging him to drop them like a hot potato) gnawing an immense mass out of the mountain-side, causing the hole now called 'The Devil's Bit,' and flying away with it. Finding, however, he was hotly pursued by St. Patrick, he spat it out where the Rock of Cashel now stands ; and on this rock, to purify it after the defilement of the arch fiend's mouth, the beautiful Cathedral of Cashel (now an interesting ruin) was built.

Archdeacon Wood thinks that the strange out-of-the-way position of Over church may be accounted for by the supposition that it was erected there for the convenience of the Earl of Chester, who occasionally resided on his Manor of Darnhall.

Verse 16. 'And oft, 'tis said, the passing bell,' &c.—In an old English homily we find— 'At the death of a manne, three belles shulde be ronge as his knigll, in worscheppe of the Trinetee ; and for a womanne, who was the secunde persone of the Trinetee, two belles shulde be rungen.' In addition to the intention of the 'passing bell' afforded by Durandus as above, it has been thought that it was rung to drive away the evil spirits, supposed to stand at the foot of the bed ready to seize the soul that it might 'gain start.' Wynkyn de Worde, in his 'Golden Legend,' speaks of the dislike of spirits to bells.

Verse 23. 'They raise to great St. Chad a prayer.'—Over church is dedicated to St. Chad.

Lord Delamere has recently built a beautiful new church in the middle of Over, to the very great convenience of the inhabitants, in memory of the late Lady Delamere.

Prophecy relating to *Beeston* Castle.

[Lelande, or Laylande, an eminent English antiquary, in his poem on the birth of Edward VI. speaks of this castle as a ruin, when he makes Fame alight on its summit and foretell its restoration.]

EXPLICUIT dehinc Fama suas perniciter alas,
    Altaque fulminei petiit *Jovis* atria victrix,
    Circuiens liquidi spatiosa volumina cœli.
      Tum quoqu e despexit terram sublimis, ocellos
      Sidereos figens Bisduni in mœnia castri, &c. &c.

Thus referred to by Bishop Gibson in his edition of Camden:—

    Randal returning from the *Syrian* land,
    This castle raised his country to defend,
    The borderer to fight and to command.
    Though ruined here the stately fabric lies,
    Yet with new glories it again shall rise,
    If I a prophet may believe old prophecies.

The following is a translation of the same prophecy, with the signature R.W., from Pennant's Journey from Chester to London :—

    Thence to *Jove*'s palace she prepared to fly,
    With outstretched pinions, through the yielding sky ;
    Wide o'er the circuit of the ample space,
    Surveyed the subject, earth, and human race.

Sublime in air, she cast her radiant eyes
Where far-famed *Beeston*'s airy turrets rise :
High on a rock it stood, whence all around
Each fruitful valley and each rising ground
In beauteous prospect lay : these scenes to view,
Descending swift, the wondering goddess flew.
Perched on the topmost pinnacle she shook
Her sounding plumes, and thus in rapture spoke :—
  ' From Syrian climes the conquering *Rando ph* came,
Whose well-fought fields bear record of his name ;
To guard his country and to check his foes,
By *Randolph*'s hands this glorious fabric rose.
Though now in ruined heaps thy bulwarks lie,
Revolving time shall raise those bulwarks high ;
If faith to ancient prophecies be due,
Then *Edward* shall thy pristine state renew.

There has long been a traditionary belief amongst the peasantry in that neighbourhood that the ancient Castle of Beeston will some day be restored to its pristine glories. The prophecy may be considered as partially realised by the building of Peckforton Castle on a neighbouring height, by John Tollemache, M.P., the owner of Beeston.

The Legend of *Bebington* Spire.

I.

IVY ! thou art fresh and young,
Gleaming in the morning sun :
In thee change is never seen,
Through the year an evergreen.

II.

When at banquet held on high,
The maid *Kissos* merrily
Danced, and *Bacchus* oft embraced,
As midst gods she wanton raced.

III.

Whilst she frolicked up and down,
Down she sank upon the ground ;
Exhausted, closed her eyes in death,
Panting fled her fluttering breath.

IV.

Ivy sprang up round the maid,
By the Greeks hence named ('tis said)
Kissos, which the oak entwines,
As *Kissos* once, the god of wines.

V.

Ivy, though so bright and green,
Oft near death is met, I ween ;
Midst th' old castle's ruins creeps,
From winding-sheet of snow-wreath peeps.

VI.

Throws its tendrils round the oak,
Which its fond embraces choke ;
Like the snake-encircling coils,
Whelming hapless prey in toils.

VII.

Ivy twined with gloomy yew,
Too oft meets the mourner's view ;
Slowly following the dead
To their last cold churchyard bed.

VIII.

Hast thou heard what hast been said
By seer *Nixon*, prophet dread ?
Of *Bebington*'s high-soaring spire
Thus he spoke in words of fire.

NIXON'S PROPHECY.

IX.

' When that spire's vane shall clasp
Ivy with its fatal grasp,
Then the last stern trumpet's call
Live and dead shall summons all.

X.

'Then shall hap the crash of doom ;
Then the dead shall burst the tomb ;
Together crushed the world shall roll,
Like a parched, flame-shrivelled scroll ! '

XI.

Many years since then have passed,
Still the world and spire last ;
Nor yet th' ivy's fatal grasp
Dares the fatal point to clasp.

XII.

Once it almost reached the height,
Filling *Cheshire* with affright ;
When the lightning's scorching blast,
Through the threatening ivy past.

XIII.

Twice since then in utmost need,
Chance hath baulked the ivy's greed ;
Still the tendrils seek the sky,
Struggling towards the spire on high.

MORAL.

XIV.

May our hearts to heaven rise,
Then we ne'er shall fear surprise ;
E'en should th' ivy top the spire,
And the doomed world wrap in fire.

Nixon is said to have prophesied that when ivy topped the Bebington spire, the end of the world would be at hand.

> The iuie greene that dothe dispised growe,
> And none doth plante, or trimme the same at all,
> Althoughe a while it spreades it selfe belowe,
> In time it mountes, with creepinge vp the wall.
>   So, thoughe the worlde the vertuous men dispise,
>   Yet vp alofte in spite of them they rise.
>
> From *Geoffrey Whitney's Emblems.*

Ballad of *Lord Delamere.*

GOOD people, give attention, a story you shall hear,
It is of the king and my lord *Delamere*;
The quarrel it arose in the Parliament House,
Concerning some taxations going to be put in
Ri toora loora la.   [force.

Says my lord *Delamere* to his majesty soon,
'If it please you, my liege, of you I'll beg a boon.'
'Then what is your boon? let me it understand.'
''Tis to have all the poor men you have in your land;
And I'll take them to *Cheshire*, and there I will sow
Both hempseed and flaxseed, and them all in a row.
Why, they'd better be hanged and stopped soon their breath,
If it please you, my liege, than to starve them to death.'

Then up starts a French lord, as we do hear,
Saying, 'Thou art a proud *Jack*,' to my lord *Delamere*;
'Thou oughtest to be stabbed'—then he turned him about—
'For affronting the king in the Parliament House.'
Then up starts His Grace the Duke of *Devonshire*,
Saying, 'I'll fight in defence of my lord *Delamere*.'

Ballad of *Lord Delamere.*

Then a stage was erected ; to battle they went :
To kill or to be killed was our noble duke's intent.
The very first push, as we do understand,
The duke's sword he bended it back in his hand.
He waited awhile, but nothing he spoke,
Till on the king's armour his rapier he broke.

The English lord who by that stage did stand,
Threw *Devonshire* another, and he caught it in his hand ;
'Play low for your life, brave *Devonshire* !' said he ;
'Play low for your life, or a dead man you'll be !'
Devonshire dropped on his knee, and gave him his death-wound.
Oh ! then that French lord fell dead upon the ground.
The king called his guards, and unto them did say,
'Bring *Devonshire* down, and take the dead man away.'

'No, if it please you, my liege—no, I've slain him like a man ;
I'm resolved to see what clothing he has got on.
Oh, fie upon your treachery ! your treachery !' said he.
'Oh king ! 'twas your intention to take my life away ;
For he fought in your armour, whilst I have fought in bare :
The same thou shalt win, king, before thou doth it wear.'

Then they all turned back to the Parliament House,
And the nobles made obeisance with their hands in their mouths.
God bless all the nobles we have in our land,
And send the Church of *England* may flourish still and stand :
For I've injured no king, no kingdom, and no crown,
But I wish that every honest man may enjoy their own.

The origin of the quarrel was supposed to have been some corn-law debate.

The title of Lord Delamere was conferred by Charles II. on Sir George Warrington.

Lord Delamere is described by a contemporary versifier as

> Fit to assist to pull a tyrant down,
> But not to please a prince that mounts the throne.

George Harry, fifth Earl of Stamford, was created in 1796 Baron De la Mere—the title enjoyed by his maternal grandfather ; and it is one of the two baronies still held by the Earl of Stamford and Warrington.

The ballad is evidently fragmentary, and very imperfect.

The Landlady of the Blue Posts Inn, *Chester*.

A tale of the reign of Bloody Mary.

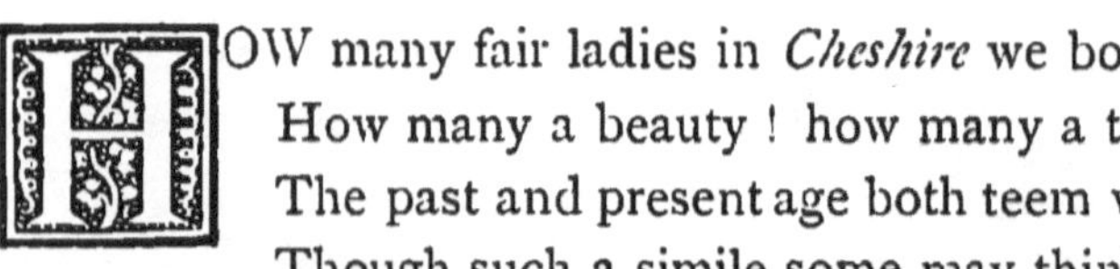

OW many fair ladies in *Cheshire* we boast !
How many a beauty ! how many a toast !
The past and present age both teem with Venuses :
Though such a simile some may think heinous is.
But the muse above all of one would fain sing,
'Tis not 'lady *Done*' to your notice I'd bring.
Though fair to a proverb that *Done* must have been,
Most beauteous lady that ever was seen !
Nor dame *Mary Cholmondeley* is now in my mind,
By James I. styled, as in annals we find,
'Bold ladye of *Cheshire !*' so much was he struck
By all he had heard of her Amazon pluck ;
Asserting her rights, confounding the lawyers,
Who tried but in vain to be her top sawyers.
No, I speak of a mistress of humble degree,
'*Elizabeth Mottershed*,' landlady she
Of Blue Posts in *Bridge* Street, where now you will find
Brittain, dealer in measures, not of ale and wine.

His is not the cuckoo cry, ' Measures, not men ! '
Whoever goes there will find ' measures for men.'
    To return to my tale : 'twas in Queen *Mary*'s days—
I am sorry I cannot say aught in her praise—
Bloody *Mary !* who to please her husband was fain
(A husband, bad luck to him who came from *Spain.'*)
Her subjects to roast (who upon religion
Might differ from her) as we should a pigeon ;
From *Spain* brought her consort the Auto-da-fé,
Which never in *England* was seen till that day.
'Twas thought that the English (the unburnt part) would love
The Roman religion; could they but just prove
It had cost them father, a child, or an aunt,
Or frizzled a husband, or wife recusant :
That heretics all would their errors forsake
When they saw those they loved most fast chained to the stake.
Alas ! through the length and the breadth of the land
Stalked legalised murder, the torture, and brand !
Ah ! say, were those *Wisemen* who dreamt they might hope
That fear would make Englishmen follow the *Pope ?*
In spite of the king, queen, and that demon *Bonner*
(A wretch, deaf to pity, compassion, and honour), ·
Still thousands were found who'd not crouch to the *Pope*,
But dared in the Bible to place their sole hope.
A *stake* in our country we all like to own—
We may all like a beefsteak ; but the torrid zone
Of *stake* (piled with faggots), to which one is chained,
(To please any Spaniard or king who e'er reigned),
We Englishmen, born under temperate skies,
Cannot relish at all ; we don't think it nice.

Once I heard of a grocer give up killing flies,
For he said that at length he found, to his surprise,
That each fly he killed lured ten to its funeral,
And sadly he feared that they'd eat his sugar all.
But Queen *Mary* persisted in bigoted spite,
Swore still that for heretics fires she *would* light,
And thought that thus Protestant hearts she'd affright.
But fast as poor martyrs in tortures expire,
More Protestants spring up, like sparks from the fire.
Yet though hundreds from home to the furnace she bore,
Still savage old *Jezebel* hungered for more ;
Resolved e'en to *Ireland* to send a commission,
Where naught should be done without Papal permission ;
And on Dr. *Cole*, who was Dean of St. *Paul's*,
Her choice as her Irish commissioner falls.
We must be exact.   This commission bore date
One thousand five hundred and eke fifty-eight,
When *Saul*, ' breathing death,' to *Damascus* was sent,
And on the destruction of Christians was bent.
His commission was framed much in the same way,
To bind men and women and drag them away.
Dr. *Cole* started off on his mission of blood,
And stopped at the Blue Posts at *Chester* for food.
  The ale wife was then one *Betsy Mottershed*,
And soon for the dean a refection she spread.
The dean asked to dinner the mayor as his guest,
Who with *Cole* to dine, his great pleasure expressed.
They ate and they drank.   As the feast 'gan to wane,
The dean with his guest confidential became ;
Dame *Mottershed* listening, chanced heard him say,
' I'll tell you a secret : this case, by my fay

(As he spoke, on a small box his fist made a dash),
'Contains what all Protestant Irish will lash.'
These words at once roused *Bessy Mottershed*'s fears
(Most women but her would have burst into tears).
She'd a brother in *Dublin*, and took it most ill,
That *Cole* might chance make of this brother a grill,
As they made of *George Marsh*, whose trial was brought on
A few years before when they burnt him in *Boughton*,
And who, when surrounded by flames at the stake,
Still boldly refused his own creed to forsake.
Oh ! what could she do her loved brother to save?
What will not a woman for mercy's sake brave ?

As *Cole* left the room the mayor to bid godeen,
Quick she opened the box without being seen,
Slipped out the commission, in which bloody *Mary*
Of Protestant blood warned *Cole* not to be chary,
And gave him full licence to bind, burn, or slay,
All those who from the *Pope* of *Rome* went astray.
As the dame from the box the commission withdrew,
A pack of cards into it quickly she threw,
The knave of hearts uppermost, to herself said,
'Exchange is no robbery,' *Bess Mottershed*.
For *Ireland* sailed *Cole*, having put back the box
Safe in his portmantle—the cunning old fox !
Nor dreamt that away his commission was flown,
And that by a woman his deanship was done.
In state at the castle the council are met ;
Cole chuckled, 'These Irish are now in my net.'
'Produce your commission :' *Cole* opened the box
(That all his proceedings might be orthodox).
Hollo ! where's the commission ? Alas ! it was gone,

The knave of hearts' red face upon them all shone.
In vain *Cole* protested, ' My mission was this,
That Protestant Irish should all in flames hiss.
Oh ! say, my lord deputy, what *shall* I do ?'
' Return,' said *Fitzwalter*, ''tis all that's left you ;
You 've nothing to do but to *London* haste back ;
And during your absence we'll shuffle the pack.'
You may fancy the feelings of good Dr. *Cole* ;
He looked not at all like a ' merry old soul ; '
But first hummed and hawed, then turned pale as an ash.
' Day carbone notanda ! I've made a sad hash ! '
He feared all his travelling bills they'd disallow ;
He thought of the waves—his face looked like tallow ;
The wind it was adverse : *Cole* recrossed the seas
(No steamers then raced 'gainst the tide and the breeze,
Like swift hunters galloping over the lea),
When at last back in *England*, who sadder than he ?
He found to his grief bloody *Mary* was dead !
Plans of burning all Protestants with her were fled.
Long, long, may the Blue Posts be sung of by fame !
Long *Chester* shall boast *Betty Mottershed*'s name,
Who saved all the Protestant Irish from flame.
Who can e'er forget this bold Protestant dame !
Forty pounds every year, be it more, be it less,
She as pension received for her deed from Queen *Bess*.

Line 6. ''Tis not Lady Done,' &c.—' As fair as Lady Done,' is an old Cheshire proverb.
She was the wife of Sir John Done, half-bow bearer of the forest of Delamere.   The
Cheshire nurses of former days used the term of ' Lady Done ' to their little girls to
express unsurpassable perfection, as they did the name of ' Lord Derby ' to their male
nurslings for the same purpose.   Mr. Ormerod, who possesses a series of original portraits

of Lady Done, her husband, and daughters, tells me he thinks ' Lady Done's impressive-ness must have arisen more from mind and manner than any unusual *personal* beauty.'

Line 9. 'Nor Dame Mary Cholmondeley,' &c.   Dame Mary Cholmondeley (heiress of the Holfords), celebrated for her long and obstinate lawsuits in defence of her property.

Line 39. 'And that demon Bonner,' &c.—Bonner, or Boner, said to have been the natural son of George Savage, rector of Davenham in Cheshire, certainly seems to have inherited the quality of his reputed father's name.   He was made Bishop of London by Henry VIII., and is known and infamous for his cruelties to the Protestants in the reign of bloody Mary.   He was very fat, corpulent, and merciless, which made some one say of him, ' That he was full of guts, and empty of bowels.'

Line 59. ' Still savage old Jezebel.'—The coins bearing Philip and Mary's impress went by the name of Ahab and Jezebel.   One shilling of that reign has the Queen's head on one side, and Philip's on the other ; on another coin the busts face each other in profile on the same side, alluded to by Butler :

> Still amorous, fond, and willing,
> Like Philip and Mary on a shilling.

Line 84. ' She'd a brother in Dublin,' &c.—His name was John Edmunds.

Line 86. ' As they made of George Marsh,' &c.—George Marsh was burnt as a hereti at Boughton, near Chester, A.D. 1554.   A rescue was attempted, after he had refused to accept a pardon, conditional on recantation.   His ashes were collected and buried in the Chapel of St. Giles in the Spital Boughton.

Line 92. ' As Cole left the room,' &c.—Dr. Henry Cole was born at Godskill in the Isle of Wight (in the churchyard of which town there are several old tombstones to a family of the name of Cole).   When Edward VI. came to the throne he embraced the Reformation, but altering his mind, resigned his preferments.   On Queen Mary's acces-sion he became a zealous Roman Catholic.   In 1554 he was made Provost of Eton, in 1556, Dean of St. Paul's.   On Queen Elizabeth's accession he was deprived of his deanery, fined 500 marks, and imprisoned.   He died in 1579.   He is called by Strype ' a person more earnest than wise.'

Line 106. ' In state at the castle,' &c.—Dublin Castle.

Line 115.   ' Return, said Fitzwalter.'—He was the Lord Deputy who is said to have used this expression to Dr. Cole.

Line 119. ' He looked not at all like a merry old soul.'—An old English ballad begins

> Old King Cole was a merry old soul,
> And a merry old soul was he, &c.

Line 121. ' Day carbone notanda !' &c.—The Romans called a lucky day one ' Cretâ notanda,' marked with chalk, and the reverse ' Carbone notanda,' or one marked with charcoal.

The scene of this story in Chester, the Blue Posts Inn, is now a shop, and was tenanted by a tailor of the name of Brittain (*vide* line 18) when this was written (1857).   It is in Bridge Street, not far from the Cross ; it has been modernised since the days of Bess Mottershed, but the room where Dean Cole's commission was exchanged for a pack of cards is still shown.   It has an old-fashioned ceiling.

' Ah! say, were they wisemen.'—When this was written Cardinal Wiseman was alive.

Old May Song.

I.

E'RE come for to bring good news in the spring,
Good news if you wish for to hear ;
Kind heaven can tell how all things go well :
We're in hopes of a plentiful year.

II.

The cold frost and snow, you very well know,
Hath pinched your cattle full sore ;
Oh ! we'd have you beware in the spring of the year,
And provide for cold winter once more.

III.

The lark he doth rise higher up to the skies,
Until he doth quite disappear ;
Then he hovers his wings, and delightfully sings,
Most pleasant and charming to hear.

IV.

Here's the little primrose ; how sweetly it grows
On ev'ry green bank of the field !
And the lily so fair, to which none can compare,
To the little primrose it must yield.

V.

The mountains, you know, have been covered with snow,
  But now they're so fresh and so gay ;
Take a leaf from the tree, and you plainly will see
  Where lies the true spirit of May.

VI.

Your lands shall be tilled, and your barns shall be filled ;
  Our Lord God so dearly provides ;
The meadows are spread with a mantle of green,
  And bordered with flowers besides.

VII.

Your maids with your flocks rise up in your smocks,
  And hasten your true love away,
Else your mistress awake, and you in your bed take,
  Whilst we are a-gathering our May.

VIII.

Our May we can gather in summer's fine weather,
  Give every one two and above ;
The more you do give, the more you will have,
  And God will you certainly love.

IX.

You young men and boys, it is high time to rise,
  For mornings grow warm in the spring ;
Take the horse and the hound, and search the wood round,
  Make the rocks and the valleys to ring.

X.

The time draweth near that we must be gone,
For we have but a short time to stay,
To dance and to sing, and to welcome the spring,
And to welcome the sweet month of May.

OLD MAY SONG.

Bluecap's Grave.

BLUECAP's remains, his dust and Bone,
Lie midst that meadow, green and Lone ;
Untired in speed he won his Urn,
E'en harder than most heroes Earn.
Cheshire will never fox-hound Call
Amongst her pack, that's better, All
Perfection, write on *Bluecap*'s Pall.

Bluecap's grave is on a meadow near Sandiway Head. He won the celebrated match for 500 guineas. For particulars, *vide* Daniel's 'Rural Sports,' vol. i. p. 211.

Inscription on a Mirror.

[Presented by R. E. Warburton to the Ladies' Cloak Room at Knutsford Ball Room.
Jan. 14, 1857.]

FAIR dancers ! since the privilege is mine,
A gift to place in that forbidden shrine,
Take with the gift the giver's caution too,
Gaze on yourself as we shall gaze on you.
While on your neck the circling jewels lie,
Dimmed by the smile that sparkles in your eye,
While the fresh bouquet, in your fingers held,
Sees its own roses by your lips excelled ;
E'er with rash step ye mingle in the dance,
Fix on that mirror your observant glance.
May future ages see reflected there,
Forms half as graceful, features half as fair !
Let the prest glove cling closely to the hand ;
Snap the gold clasp, the ivory fan expand ;
Smooth the full skirt, adjust the pliant shoe ;
Each point, each fold, fastidiously review.
So shall no rent the *Brussel*'s lace impair,
Though jealous pangs the inward bosom tear ;
So shall the gown, through gallops and quadrille,
Though hearts be crushed, remain unruffled still.
Go ! partners wait, impatient for the ball,
Go ! smiling go ! and bliss attend you all.

The *Marler's* Song.

I.

E are the boys to fey a pit,
And then yoe good marl out of it
For them who'd grow a good turmit.
Chorus.

Who-whoop, Wo-whoop, wo—o—o—o—o
(Three times repeated).

II.

If marler should to shirk work oss,
We hold him a tit's back across ;
The lazy chap we mun well poss.
Chorus, Who-whoop &c.

III.

When some one comes from the great ha',
Who never marling saw before,
He'll listen to the marlers' ca'.
Chorus, Who-whoop &c.

IV.

Our lord from him will lorgesse take ;
To him our thanks he'll reetly make,
Whilst we shout till our sides do ache.
      Chorus, Who-whoop &c.

V.

Quoth he, ' Part of five thousand pounds
A gent hath geen us; one half-crown
True marlers we to shout are bound.
      Chorus, Who-whoop &c.

VI.

At the week's end we all will meet,
Where we know that the liquor's reet,
And there we'll drink into the neet.
      Chorus, Who-whoop &c.

VII.

When from the public we turn out
In ring, the gang begins, no doubt,
The lorgesse nomines to shout.
      Chorus, Who-whoop &c.

VIII.

But we must of one thing take heed,
Lest slip should chance at the marl head,
And we then all be crushed stark dead.
      Chorus, Who-whoop &c.

IX.

When shut the pit, the labour o'er,

He whom we work for opes his door,

And gees to us of drink galore,

For this was always *Marler's* law.

Chorus, Who-whoop, Who-whoop, wo—o—o—o—o

(Three times repeated).

An old saying in Cheshire is, 'He who marls sand may buy the land.' In all old leases Cheshire tenants were bound annually to marl part of their farm. The first process in marling is to *fey* the pit, i.e. to remove the surface to get at the marl which is under it.

To *yoe*, spelt as pronounced, evidently a provincialism for to hew or cut out with the spade. *Pit*, marl-pit. *Turmit*, turnip. To *oss* is to offer to do.

To poss is the punishment used by marlers to any lazy marler or teamsman. He is pulled down upon a horse's back, spread out, and beaten with the flat of the marlers' spades, where it will injure him least. *Ha'*, hall. *The lord of the pit*, the head marler of the gang, who, amongst other things, receives any lorgesse, and accounts for it. *Lorgesse* (evidently a corrupted synonym of largesse), the present made to marlers.

Stanza 5. 'Part of 5000*l.*' &c.—The lord of the pit always announces to his fellows any sum given as lorgesse of 2*s.* 6*d.* and upwards as 'part of 5000*l.*' under 2*s.* 6*d.* the lorgesse is announced as part of 500*l.* *Geen*, means given ; *reet*, right ; *neet*, night. *Shout*, the peculiar note used when the marlers cry out the lorgesse and the nominee, i.e. the name of the donor ; it is a long prolonged drawl, followed by the chorus of Who-whoop, &c.

Stanza 7. Ring is the circle in which marlers stand before they begin to shout. *Gang*, the party that undertake a marl-pit. *Marl head*, the deepest part of the pit, where the bank occasionally slips in upon the gang.

Stanza 9. 'When shut the pit,' &c.—Shutting a pit is finishing the contracted work. There are many other terms used in marling. The *shoulders* of the pit, i.e. the sides. A *midfeather* is a bank left between two pits.

The old marl-pits through Cheshire are very frequently the only watering-places for the cattle. The useless pits during the last generation of improvement have been generally filled up; but three, four, or more pits may still be seen in several of the farms, even in one field. I read the above lines to an old tenant, a marler of former days, as a marling song ; and he said, 'It's all reet, it's all reet, but I wonder au never heard that song before.'

Patriotic Verses on Inn Signs at *Middlewich.*

The date evidently the time of the menaced French invasion from Boulogne.

I.

HEN folks meet together dissension to sow,
And by breeding divisions encourage the foe,
When false motives like colours they hold to our
view,
'Tis a sign they might find something better to do.

II.

If ever the French should attempt to come here
To eat up our beef and to drink our strong beer,
Of both they'd fall short, but if fighting they wished,
At each sign of Middlewich they would be dished.

III.

First the Lion called 'Golden' would make them to quake,
And the 'Talbot,' I doubt not, would give them a shake;
At the sign of the 'Wolf,' would they venture to rap,
They'd find, though too late, they'd run into a trap.

IV.

By our Bears White and Black they'd be put to the rout,
And a threshing they'd get at the 'Wheat Sheaf,' no doubt ;
From 'Lord *Hood*,' a broadside they'd meet, to their cost ;
And at the 'Bull's Head' they'd be savagely tost.

V.

At the 'White and Red Lion,' they'd find, to their shame,
Whether black, white, or blue, British Lions are game ;
At the 'Bridge Foot' they'd stop, and perhaps call for a whet ;
And they'd get it—that is a good ducking they'd get.

VI.

If they call at the 'White Horse,' they'll treat them so kind,
With a horseshoe, that more kicks than halfpence they'll find ;
Should they venture to peep at the 'George and the Dragon,'
They'd see, to their cost, they'd got nothing to brag on.

VII.

Next at the 'Seven Stars,' they'd soon show them the door ;
At the 'Oak' a good drubbing they'd get, and no more,
Should these 'Sans-culottes' dare with our 'Crown' interpose,
They'll prick their French fingers well under the 'Rose.'

VIII.

At the 'Nag's Head' with bites and cuffs they would be treated,
At the 'Ring o' Bells' next with an empty house greeted ;
The sign of the 'Eagle' would raise fresh alarms,
And they'd run like soup maigre to escape the 'King's Arms.'

IX.

May the sign of the 'King' ever meet with respect,
And our good constitution each Briton protect ;
May he who first caused all the troubles of *France*,
Be high hung on a sign, on nothing to dance.

Stanza 3. Talbot, old name for Mastiff.

THE DRAGON OF MOSTON.

The Dragon of *Moston*.

I.

FT have we heard of that fell fight,
In which old *England*'s patron knight,
By chroniclers St. *George* who's hight
    The scaly dragon slew.

II.

But of that combat now I sing,
With which all *Cheshire* once did ring ;
A picture of the fight I'll fling,
    And of a warrior true.

III.

A dragon *Cheshire* troubled sore,
Insatiate was his horrid maw ;
Clotted with blood and poisonous gore,
    Wide wasted he the land.

IV.

Widows and orphans would turn pale,
Were he but named, men's hearts would fail ;
Warriors, ne'er known before to quail,
    Durst not before him stand.

V.

Moston's curst township rued the day
When in its swamp it wallowing lay ;
Like the thick dust uprose the spray,
　　As thrashed his tail the slime.

VI.

Remnant of monsters, that the flood
Retiring left (a deadly brood),
Or sprung from some gaunt giant's blood,
　　Spawn of some devilish time.

VII.

Sharp fangs gaped wide a triple row,
Its bloodshot eyes like flames did glow,
Its body like a serpent low,
　　And scaled o'er as with mail.

VIII.

Six claws on either side appear,
Its prey to seize, its prey to tear :
'Twas said, that e'en a grizzly bear
　　Had crushed its whelming tail.

IX.

Where'er it roamed, its upas breath
On all sides, round, above, beneath,
Like plague-sores, belched a horrid death,
　　'Gainst which 'twas vain to pray.

X.

This gallant *Venables* did hear
(A man he was to *Cheshire* dear),
And *Moston* he resolved to clear,
    Or perish in the fray.

XI.

He vowed unto his ladye fair
To beard the dragon in his lair,
And offered up to heaven a prayer
    To grant him strength in fight.

XII.

The dragon's swamp scarce had he won,
The beast had seized a widow's son;
He was his mother's only one.
    Loud shouted then the knight.

XIII.

The morning mists that challenge cleft;
The dragon heard the shout, and left
The child of sense not life bereft,
    And rushed on in his might.

XIV.

Bold *Venables* unflinching drew
With steady hand the sounding yew;
Forth, winged by death, the arrow flew,
    And pierced the dragon's eye.

XV.

Well 'twas he aimed not at his side :
The sharpest bolt had vainly tried
To pierce elsewhere his scale-armed hide,
    Or to the heart come nigh.

XVI.

Fierce through the reeds the dragon crashed,
The swamp to foam in fury lashed,
Wildly at *Venables* it dashed :
    The knight ne'er dreamt to fly.

XVII.

On the blind side advanced he then,
And smote the beast once and again
Between the scales : soon in the fen
    Black heart blood soaked the ground.

XVIII.

Far, far, that dying shriek was heard,
E'en distant *Beeston*'s warders stirred,
And springing up some onslaught feared,
    So awful was the sound.

XIX.

Who, who, may paint the widow's joy ?
Again, again, she hugs her boy.
What can the mother now annoy ?
    Her lost child breathes again !

XX.

Broad lands in *Moston* for that deed
(Fortune's reward, and Valour's meed),
For *Cheshire* saved in utmost need,
 The *Venables* did gain.

XXI.

But what than lands he valued mair,
Was a dark tress of glossy hair
(For this, what would not true knight dare ?),
 Gift of his ladye fair.

XXII.

A dying dragon bathed in gore,
Which e'en in death an infant tore,
In arms he proudly thenceforth bore,
 Emblazoned on his shield.

XXIII.

Still, children at the dragon quake ;
The fight to list they'll play forsake ;
Still by the name of ' *Dragon*'s lake '
 Is called that *Moston* field.

Ancient *Cheshire* Games.

Circa 1600.

Auntient customes in games used by boys and girles merily set out in verse.

MANY they dare challenge for to throw the sleudge,
  To jump or leap over ditch or hedge,
  To wrastle, play at stooleball, or to runne,
  To pick the barre, or to shoote off a gonne,
To play at loggets, nineholes, or ten pinnes,
To trye it out at footeballe by the shinnes,
At ticke jacke, Irish, noddy, maw, and ruffe,
At hott cockley, leape frogge, or blindman's buffe,
To drinke halph potts, or deale at the whole can,
To play at chesse, or pen and inkhorn *John*,
To daunce the morris play at barley breake,
At all exployts a man can thinke or speake.
At shove groate, venterpoynte, or cross and pile,
At beshrow him that's last at any style,
At leapinge ore a Christmas eve bonefier,
Or at the drawinge donne out of the myer,
At shoote cocke, gregory stooleball, and what not,
Pickepoynt topp, and scourge to make them hott.

Stoolcballc. An ancient game of ball played by both sexes. According to Dr. Johnson, it is a game where a ball is driven from stool to stool. In Lewis' 'English Presbyterian

Eloquence,' p. 17, talking of the tenets of the Puritans, he observes that all games were strictly forbidden where there is any hazard of loss, not so much as a game of stoolball for a tansay (a sort of cake). In Herrick's ' Hesperides' we find

> At stoolball, Lucia, let us play
>   For sugar, cakes, and wine,
> Or for a tansie let us pay ;
>   The losse be thine or mine.
> If thou, my deere, a winner be
>   At trundling of the balle,
> The wager thou shalt have, and me,
>   And my misfortunes all.

To picke the barre, means the same as pitching or flinging the bar.

Loggets or *Loggats*, an old game, forbidden by statute in Henry VIII.'s time. It is thus played, according to Steevens :—A stake is fixed in the ground ; those who play throw loggats at it ; he that is nearest the stake wins. Loggats are small pieces of wood thrown at fruit that cannot otherwise be got at. Loggats, little logs or wooden pins, a play the same with ninepins ; in which boys, however, often used bones instead of wooden pins.

Dean Milles' M.S., Halliwell's Dictionary.

Nineholes, according to Forby, is a game for which you make nine round holes in the ground, and a ball is aimed at them from a certain distance : or the holes are made in a board with a number over each, through which the ball is to pass. Nares thinks it is the same with ninemens morris, called in some places ninepenny mail.

Tick Jack, a kind of backgammon ; so is *Irish. Noddy*, a game at cards, by some supposed to have been the same as cribbage. *Mawe* was also a game of cards, played by any number from two to six, with a piquet pack of thirty-six cards. *Ruffe* was also a game of cards, at which ' the greatest sorte of the sute carrieth away the game.'

Hott Cockley is of course identical with Hot Cockles.

Pen and Inkhorn John.

Barley Break, an ancient rural game.

Shove Groate, identical with Shovel Board.

Cross and Pile, heads and tails ; tossing.

Venterpoynt, a child's game.

Beshrowe or *Beshrewe*, a mild form of imprecation. Florio derives the word from shrew-mouse, to which deadly qualities were once ascribed.

Topp and Scourge, a whipping-top.

The *Gayton* Wishing Well.

[It is thought in the neighbourhood of Gayton, that anyone who may here form a wish,
and throw a stone backwards into the well, will ensure the realisation of their desires.]

I.

THE Wishing Well, the Wishing Well,
  In *Gayton* lane you find;
Oft had I of the spring heard tell,
  Sought by fond maid or hind.

II.

Should ought fair maiden long to have,
  She flies to this lone spot;
She throws a stone into the wave,
  Then seeks again her cot.

III.

She fancies as the bubbles rise
  Above the sinking stone,
Her wish must realise the prize
  For which she left her home.

IV.

Look under that rock moss-grown cope
That roofs the Wishing Well ;
For there each pebble speaks of hope,
Of hundreds heaped pell-mell.

V.

And none of those who fling a stone,
And breathe fond wishes here,
But deem they thus the seeds have sown
Of fruit esteemed most dear.

VI.

Young *Nelly* trusts that from the fair
To which her *Lubin*'s gone,
He may bring back to deck her hair
Some gaud—she drops a stone.

VII.

When he that e'en returns to *Nell*,
And brings the sighed-for toy,
She's sure to stone and Wishing Well
She owes her simple joy.

VIII.

Too oft we think we victims are
Of disappointments chill,
That we alone (poor martyrs) bear
The brunt of every ill.

IX.

But could we register and note
    Our granted wishes all,
Soon, soon, our discontent, I wot,
    Like blighted fruit would fall.

X.

As I thought thus and mused beside
    The *Gayton* Wishing Well,
I fancied on the wall I spied
    A strange fern in its cell.

XI.

I tore the treasure from its nook ;
    When I gazed on it near,
I cried (triumphant at my luck),
    More than I wished is here.

XII.

Thus, through life's journey we may share
    The long-sought wish, and more.
Unlooked-for joys than granted prayer,
    Are sometimes brighter far.

William III. slept at Gayton Hall on his way to Ireland. There is not, I am afraid, sufficient authority for asserting that his successes against James were owing to his having previously thrown a stone into the Wishing Well.

The *Rostherne* Bell.

I.

ERRILY, merrily, over the *Mere*,
 The echoes rose and fell ;
Rose on the breeze, fell on the ear,
 Dingdong the *Rostherne* bell.

II.

On buttress old, and crumbling stone,
 The masons plied their trade,
Repaired the courses overthrown,
 The rents that time had made.

III.

When, lo ! from battlement to base
 A shivering shakes the steeple ;
Down drops the big bell from its place,
 Right in among the people !

IV.

Down the steep bank that crowns the lake
 It crashed, and leapt, and rolled,
Through birch-wood copse, and briar, and brake,
 And 'mid the Lindens old.

V.

Till on the margin of the *Mere*,
  'Tis fain at length to settle,
Exhausted by its mad career,
  That ponderous mass of metal.

VI.

But oh the sweat, and oh the toil,
  The strain of the muscles' power,
The bursting sob, the weary coil
  To try it back to the Tower !

VII.

Quoth one in wrath : ' Thou senseless lump,
  I would the devil had you !
When at the word, with a spring and a thump,
  Back towards the lake it flew.

VIII.

First, in its headlong course, it crushed
  Th' unlucky wight who swore,
Then down the bank it madly rushed ;
  They never saw it more.

IX.

In depths unfathomable drowned,
  No more that tuneful tongue
Shall greet the ear with cheerful sound
  At morn or even song.

X.

And now whenever peal the bells
From *Rostherne's* tower so hoary,
The wailing sound too plainly tells
Of its departed glory.

Stanza 7. 'With a spring and a thump.'

Αὖτις ἔπειτα πέδονδε κυλίνδετο λᾶας ἀναιδής.

The Curst Fisherman.

A Tale of the Wirral.

[On the Cheshire coast, if anyone should find a corpse thrown up by the sea, and instead of procuring it Christian burial leave it to the mercy of the winds and waves, he would be considered to have incurred eternal opprobrium and obloquy of the most indelible nature, and that the avenging spirit of the unburied corpse will ever afterwards through life perseveringly haunt the unhappy man who disregarded the sacred rights of the dead.]

I.

WO fishermen loved *Bessy Blake* ;
 A comely maid was she ;
Her parent's cot was at *Hoylake*,
 Not far from *Hilbree.*

II.

Two fishermen loved *Bessy Blake*,
 Each other hated sair ;
Their names *John Stone* and *William Lake*,
 But *John* she favoured mair.

III.

A wild storm swept the *Cheshire* shore ;
 John Stone was on the deep ;
His boat, alas ! was seen no more,
 Which *Bessy* caused to weep.

THE CURST FISHERMAN.

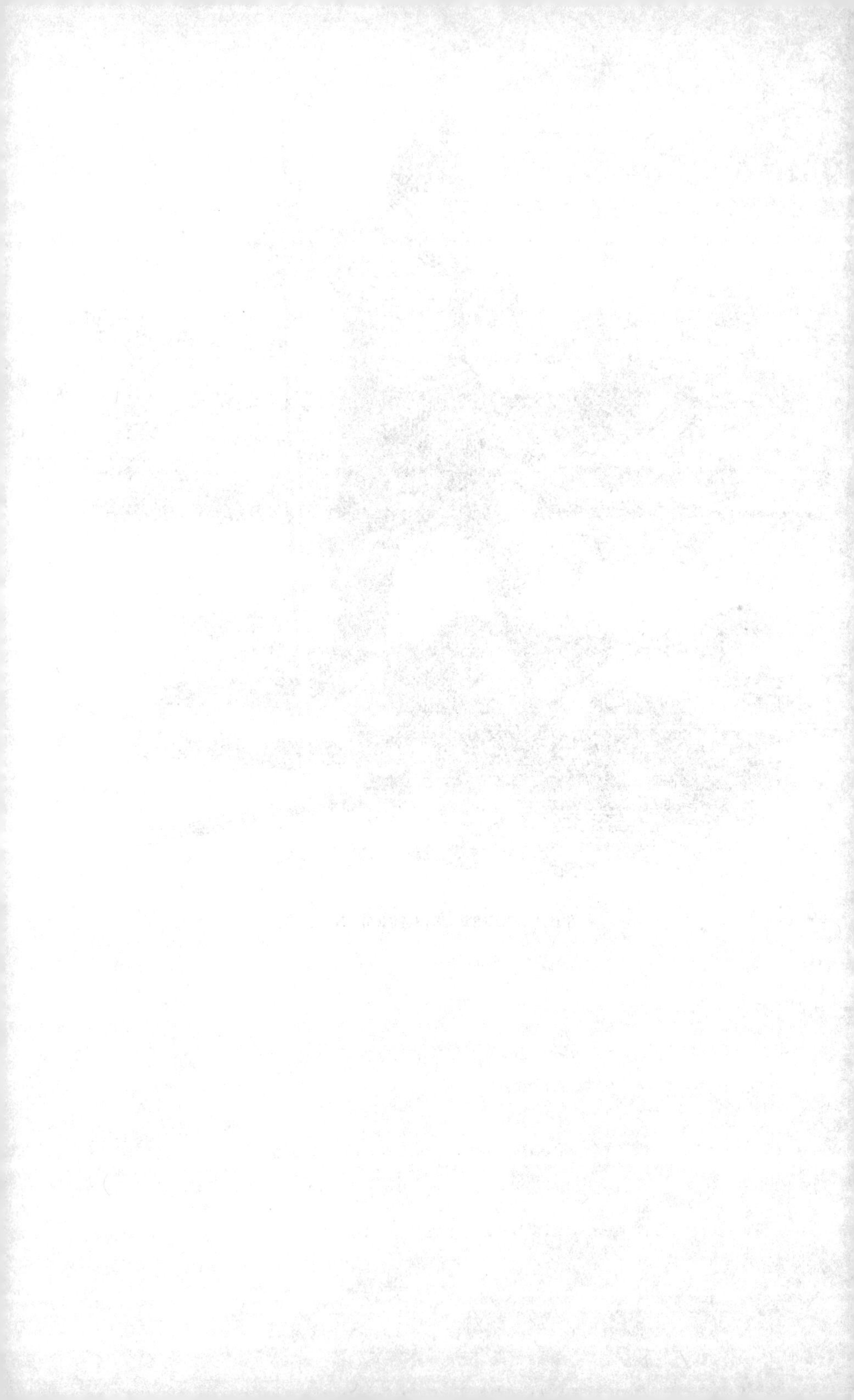

IV.

Early next morn *Will Lake* arose,
    The waste of sands he sought ;
Landwards a sight his life-blood froze,
    The flowing billows brought.

V.

His rival's corpse lay stark and stare,
    Half swathed in slimy weed !
One hand still clasped a lock of hair,
    Grasped in his utmost need.

VI.

'Twas *Bessy*'s : *Lake* turned grimly then,
    And spurned him as he lay,
And watched till the tide ebbed again,
    And whirled the corpse away.

VII.

A shrimper by an old wreck sat ;
    Unseen the deed he viewed,
Soon known by all, when general hate
    The miscreant pursued.

VIII.

Shame on the fisherman, who leaves
    A corpse the hoarse wave's sport !
Whose winding-sheet the seawrack weaves,
    And wild gulls scream the mort.

IX.

No peace had *William* from that hour,
  Within, without the door ;
His rival's face still seemed to glour,
  As when him last he saw.

X.

By *Bessy* scorned (for she'd been told
  Who'd her dead lover spurned),
Avoided by the young and old,
  Despised where'er he turned.

XI.

By night, by day, at eve, at morn,
  Still, still, those features sad
Gazed on him with that stare forlorn.
  At length the wretch went mad.

Cheshire May Song.

ALL on this pleasant evening together come are we
  For the summer springs, so fresh, green, and gay,
To tell you of a blossom that hangs on every tree,
  Drawing near to the morning of May.
Oh this is pleasant ! singing sweet May-flower is springing,
  And summer comes, so fresh and gay.

Rise up, the master of the house, all in his chain of gold,
  For the summer springs, so fresh, green, and gay,
And turn unto your loving wife, so comely to behold,
  Drawing near to the morning of May.
Oh this is pleasant ! singing sweet May-flower is springing,
  And summer comes, so fresh and gay.

Rise up, the mistress of this house, with gold upon your breast,
  For the summer springs, so fresh, green, and gay ;
And if your body's sleeping, we hope your soul has rest,
  Drawing near to the morning of May.
Oh this is pleasant ! singing sweet May-flower is springing,
  And summer comes, so fresh and gay.

or,

    Oh ! rise up, Mr. A. B. ; all joys to you betide !
    Your steed stands ready saddled a hunting for to ride.
                &c. &c. &c.

or,

    Your saddle is of silver, your bridle is of gold ;
    Your bride shall ride beside you, all lovely to behold.
                &c. &c. &c.

or,

    Oh ! rise up, Mr. D. C., and take your pen in hand ;
    For you're a learned scholar, as we do understand.
                &c. &c. &c.

or,

    Oh ! rise up, Mistress E. F., all in your rich attire ;
    You are to have some noble lord or else some wealthy squire.
                &c. &c. &c.

or,

    Oh ! rise up, all the little ones, the flower of all your kin,
    And blessed be the chamber their bodies lie within.
                &c. &c. &c.

or,

    Oh ! rise up, the good housekeeper, all in her gown of silk,
    And may she have a husband good and twenty cows to milk.
                &c. &c. &c.

or,

    But where are all those fair maids that used here to dance ?
    Oh, they are gone abroad from hence, to spend their lives in
                &c. &c. &c.   [*France.*

or,

　God bless your house and harbour, your riches and your store,
　　For the summer springs, so fresh and gay :
　We hope the *Lord* will prosper you both now and evermore,
　　Drawing near to this morning of May.
　Oh this is pleasant ! singing sweet May-flower is springing,
　　And summer comes, so fresh, green, and gay.

NEW MAY SONG.

The verses of the preceding song may be extended to suit the inmates, or any particular inmate, of the different houses visited on their rounds by the May Singers, and the wit and point would of course depend upon the talents, quickness, and readiness of the leader of the band.

Prince *Madoc's* Heirs.

A Legend of Farndon Bridge.

I.

RINCE *Madoc* lay upon his bier
    (The Lord of *Dinas Bran*)
At *Valle Crucis* Abbey near ;
    The monks his requiem sang.

II.

They pray for him as chief of *Yale*,
    Of *Dinas Bran* the Lord ;
Saesneg, Chirk, Nanheudwy, in *Wales*,
    And *Bromfield's* acres broad.

III.

Two sons survive, Prince *Madoc's* pride,
    His knightly name to bear,
These were his lordships to divide,
    And his estates to heir.

IV.

The eldest just ten springs had seen,
    The younger scarcely eight ;
Oh ! winsome boys they were, I ween,
    But sad their orphan fate.

V.

Better for them, poor bairns ! had they
Escaped the princely lot,
From knightly towers far away,
Born in some lonely cot.

VI.

The lordly oak uprooted lies,
That braved aloft the gale ;
Wild storms the violet defies,
Nestling in lowly vale.

VII.

King *Edward* gave them guardians two,
Their infant years to tend,
And their broad lands with honour due
From wrong and bale defend.

VIII.

These guardians both wore ermine fur ;
The Earl of *Warren* one,
The other of Lord *Mortimer*
Was, *Roger* hight, the son.

IX.

Their names were noble ; noble blood,
Alas ! ran through their veins ;
Their hearts were black and dead to good
As the first murderer *Cain's*.

R 2

X.

Like husbandmen (of whom of old
Our Saviour's story ran,
Which He to His disciples told),
They laid their treacherous plan.

XI.

'Come, let us kill the heirs,' they say,
' Their lands shall be our own ;
Their death to us opes fortune's way ;
Let it at once be done.'

XII.

Dark was the night ; black *Deva*'s bed
Ran deep with wintry flood ;
Next day some spoke of shrieks, and said
They feared some deed of blood !

XIII.

From that dread hour, no mortal eye
Prince *Madoc*'s sons e'er saw;
O'er *Dinas Bran* and *Nanheudwy*
The rule their guardians bore.

XIV.

The eye of heaven who may fly ?
Naught is from *God* concealed.
Murder, though wrought all secretly,
By heaven is oft revealed.

XV.

Belated travellers quake with fear,
  And spur their starting horse ;
For childish shrieks, they say, they hear
  As *Farndon*'s Bridge they cross.

XVI.

Two fairy forms, all clothed in white,
  Still hovering o'er the *Dee*,
At midnight oft by pale moonlight
  The ghost-struck rustics see.

Stanza 8. ' Both wore ermine fur.' Ermine and sable were furs worn as distinctive marks of nobility.

Stanza 12. ' Ran deep with wintry flood:' Turbidus hybernis forte fluebat aquis.

Sammy Grice's Epitaph.

[He was a half idiot dwarf, a citizen of Chester, who died March 1821, aged 77. He gained his livelihood by the sale of ventpegs and skewers to the brewers and butchers of Chester.]

CAPED from a world of ridicule and pains,
    This verdant copse o'erlays the brief remains
    Of *Samuel Grice*, a man of much renown
    Within the circle of his native town.
Long of that town he was the current jest,
And schoolboys struggled which should tease him best ;
His pigmy stature, waddling gait, and phiz,
Oft furnished laughter to the vacant quiz,
Whilst they who scanned him with a feeling eye
Pitied his harmless nature, and passed by.
On Sundays in his scarlet coat attired,
And reverend hat, by waggish folk admired,
Sure as the Sabbath came its weekly round
At church the harmless idiot was found ;
When done, though pleased his finery to view,
He reached his hand to welcome all he knew,
And with a smile which spoke his welcome true,
He'd gabble forth, 'Well, sir ! How do ? how do

SAMMY GRICE.

But ah! the ruthless tapster Death
Hath placed a ventpeg on poor *Sammy's* breath,
And all his little virtues could not save
His little body from this little grave,
His soul they can—his soul, to mercy given,
I trust through mercy now hath rest in heaven,
Where they who hold deformity a jest
Will ne'er intrude to mar his heavenly rest.

Chorus of Liberal-minded Foxes.

[Met to celebrate the birthday of Geoffrey Shakerley, late Master of the Cheshire Fox Hounds.]

CHORUS.

ERE'S to *Shakerley*'s health, and returns of this day,
And that we may, like him, live to see it we pray.

1st *Fox.*

Here's his health ! o'er my old wife he sounded the mort,
A. regular vixen ! one of the wrong sort.

2nd *Fox.*

Here's his health ! of my firstborn his hounds made their grub ;
His crimes whitened my tag—a most dissolute cub.

3rd *Fox, a real lady.*

Here's his health ! for he chopped my fat husband in cover ;
I'm blest with a younger mate, but older lover.

4th *Fox.*

Here 's his health ! for as panting I lay in a drain,
Having had quantum *suff* in a very long run,
He would not let them dig me, on which they were fain,
Saying, 'Leave him alone, he will show some more fun.'

CHORUS.

Here's *Shakerley's* health ! for though we may be sinners,
He saves us from keepers, and pays for our dinners ;
It is he plants our gorses so snug and so warm,
And takes care that traps and nets do us no harm ;
When they lay up their cubs he keeps our wives quiet,
Driving far from our earths all row and all riot ;
And a *brush* now and then we can very well spare,
When he gives us a brush so oft during the year.
And may many returns of his birthday be spent !
May he live to a hundred !　Who knows more of *scent ?*

There was a Jolly Miller lived on the River *Dee*.

[From the 'Convivial Songster, 1782.' The tune it was sung to was an old one called ' The Budgeon, it is a delicate trade.']

I.

THERE was a jolly Miller once lived on the river *Dee*,
He danced and sang from morn to night, no lark so blithe as he;
And this the burden of his song for ever used to be,
' I care for nobody, no not I, if nobody cares for me.'

II.

' I live by my mill, *God* bless her ! she's kindred, child, and wife.
I would not change my station for any other in life.
No lawyer, surgeon, or doctor, e'er had a groat from me.
I care for nobody, not I, if nobody cares for me.'

III.

When spring begins its merry career, oh how his heart grows gay !
No summer's drought alarms his fears, nor winter's sad decay ;
No foresight mars the Miller's joy, who 's wont to sing and say,
' Let others toil from year to year, I live from day to day.'

IV.

Thus like the Miller, bold and free, let us rejoice and sing :
The days of youth are made for glee, and time is on the wing.
This song shall pass from me to thee along this jovial ring ;
Let heart and voice and all agree to say, ' Long live the King ! '

About two years since the following version, supposed by the finder to be the original song of ' the Jolly Miller,' was found written on the fly-leaf of a volume of Dryden's Poems, printed 1716.

I.

THERE was a jolly Miller once
   Lived on the river *Dee,*
He worked and sang from morn till night,
   No lark more blithe than he ;
And this the burden of his song
   For ever used to be,
' I care for nobody, not I,
   If nobody cares for me.'

II.

The reason why he was so blithe
   He once did thus unfold,
' The bread I eat my hands have earned ;
   I covet no man's gold ;
I do not fear next quarter-day ;
   In debt to none I be.
   I care for nobody,' &c.

III.

'A coin or two I've in my purse
  To help a needy friend ;
A little I can give the poor,
  And still have some to spend.
Though I may fail, yet I rejoice
  Another's goodhap to see.
    I care for nobody,' &c.

IV.

So let us his example take,
  And be from malice free ;
Let every one his neighbour serve
  As served he'd like to be ;
And merrily push the can about,
  And drink and sing with glee.
If nobody cares a doit for us,
  Why not a doit care we.

There is an old Cheshire proverb expressive of boundless extravagance, ' If thou hadst the rent of Dee Mills thou wouldst spend it.' The Dee miller, by publishing the whole of his song, I prove to have been a very amiable character, instead of the personification of selfishness, of which I have heard him accused by those who knew nothing of him but the verse ' I care for nobody,' &c., misquoting even this line by putting an *and* instead of an *if*.

THE MILLER OF THE DEE.

The Miller of the *Dee.*

The Miller of the *Dee.*

Unica Semper Avis.

To my countrimen of the *Namptwiche* in *Cheshire*.

To the succeeding verses is prefixed the emblem of the Phœnix, from a choice of emblemes
by Geoffrey Whitney, A.D. 1586.

THE Phœnix rare, with fethers freshe of hewe,
   Arabia's righte, and sacred to the sonne,
   Whome other birdes with wonder seeme to vewe,
   Dothe live untill a thousande yeares be ronne,
Then makes a pile, which, when with sonne it burnes,
Shee flies therein, and so to ashes turnes;
Whereof behoulde! an other Phœnix rare
With speede dothe rise, most beautifull and faire.
And though for truthe this manie doe declare,
Yet thereunto I mean not for to sweare,
   Althoughe I knowe that aucthors witnes true
   What here I write, bothe of the oulde and newe ;
Which when I wayed the newe and eke the oulde,
I thought upon youre towne, destroyed with fire,
And did, in minde, the newe Namptwiche behoulde,
   A spectacle for anie man's desire,
      Whose buildinges brave, where cinders weare but late,
      Did represente (me thought) the Phœnix fate.

And as the oulde was manie hundreth yeares
  A town of fame before it felt that crosse,
Even so (I hope) this Wiche that nowe appeares
  A Phœnix age shall laste and knowe no losse.
    Which *God* vouchsafe, who make you thankfull all
    That see this rise and sawe the other fall.

The above is a specimen of Geoffrey Whitney, our oldest Cheshire poet. 'A Choice of Emblemes' was published at Leyden, in the house of Christopher Plantyn. The fire to which he alludes took place in 1583, at a brewery in Nantwich, and destroyed 600 dwelling houses, brewers' outhouses, &c., doing damage to the amount of 30,000*l.* There was a general collection for the inhabitants through the country, and the Queen subscribed 2000*l.*, and what timber might be required from Delamere Forest to rebuild the town.

Mr. Green, M.A., of Knutsford, has published a valuable reprint of Geoffrey Whitney's Emblems, or rather an exact reproduction.

'*Congleton Bear Town* where they sold the Bible to buy a Bear.'

Old Cheshire Proverb.

 LONG time ago, in our forefathers' days,
They sought for amusement in all sorts of ways,
Dog fighting ! bull baiting ! or drawing the brock !
Or losing their broad lands by backing a cock !
Then ladies of all ages raced for a smock !
Scarce any man ever went sober to bed ;
'Tis quite dreadful to think the lives they all led !
At that time in *Cheshire* no fun could compare
With that sport of all sports—viz. baiting a bear ;
Many inns of the past still tell the same tale,
For scarce in the county a hamlet will fail
To hang up as sign a bear black, white, or brown
  There's *Barton* which must of the bear be the town.
No doubt to this bear baiting we trace the cause
Why we find in *Cheshire* so many ' Bears' Paws ; '
But *Congleton* bear baiting loved above all,
Headquarters, that place, of the sport we may call ;
For old town accounts show what money they spent
In paying their bearwards, and how much more went,

S

(Three-and-sixpence) for bringing the bears to the wake,
Besides drink, the thirst of these bearwards to slake ;
But truth must be told, e'en though *Congleton* blush,
We must not all sins of our forefathers hush.
A new Bible was wanted—the old one was done—
And Bibles in those days cost a precious sum !
At length all the townsfolk resolved to subscribe,
(Expense is scarce felt which the many divide).
So at length they collect all the gold they require,
To the joy of the parson, the clerk, and the choir.
"Twas the time of the wakes, when just then 'twas said
The town bear, when he was most wanted, was dead.
How to raise a new bear ?—In these days 'twould be easy,
For if M.P., sheriff, or mayor, they would teaze ye ;
At once to subscribe, a new bear would be bought,
Or from Wombwell's or other wild beast show, be brought ;
Or a ladies' bazaar at once improvised,
That unblushing robbery, now legalised,
Which turns pincushions, penwipers, slippers, or braces,
(Forced on crabbed old gents by the fairest of faces)
To sums which are well worth anyone's robbing,
Though raised from small items, straw, tape, or bobbin ;
In those days, those modern plans were all unknown,
Of stealing a friend's purse and saving your own.

    The wakes were approaching !—and there was no bear !
Some one whispered (who 'twas none e'er dared to declare,
No one's ever wrong unless it be the cat,
Th' experience of all ages teaches us that),
' There's the money which to buy a Bible we raised,
With that buy a bear at once, for heaven be praised,

Our priest has so long read in th' old book, 'tis clear
He might do so still for at least one more year!'
Alas! human nature! the bear won the day,
So convincing the reason 'There's nothing to pay!'
A new bear was bought straight instead of the book—
The insult the parson was thus forced to brook;
In vain he cried loudly 'My townsmen forbear,
For shame! such unbearable conduct to dare!'
This sacrilege cost Congletonians dear,
Through the breadth of the county the sneer forced to hear,
(Whenever men saw Congletonian near)
'Like *Congleton* bear town, where money to save,
The Bible itself for a new bear they gave.'
P.S. The townsmen 'tis true would explain this away.
'In those days when Bibles were so dear,' they say
That they th' *old* Bible swopped at the wakes for a bear,
Having first bought a new book.' Thus shirk they the sneer,
And taunts 'gainst their town thus endeavour to clear.

Line 10. 'Many inns of the past,' &c.—Apropos to bears and inns, I have heard of the following inscription on a tavern :—

'Good *Bear* sold here, my own *Bruin.*'

Line 15. 'Why we find in Cheshire so many Bears' Paws.'—The Bear's Paw is the sign of many old-established Inns, at High Leigh and Frodsham, amongst other places.

We learn what was done in former days by what was forbidden. The Scholars and Fellows of Eton College are forbidden, amongst other things, to keep 'simiam, ursam,' &c.

Line 18. 'For old town accounts show,' &c.—In the town accounts of Congleton are the following items :—

		£	s.	d.
1589. Paid the Trafford's man the bearward	. . . .	0	4	4
1601. Gave to bearward at the great cock-fight	. . . .	0	6	8
Wine for the gentlemen at the said fight	. . . .	0	6	0
1602. Bestowed at the great bear bait in wine, sack, spice, figs, almonds, and beer	. . . .	0	11	10
1613. Fetching the bears at the wakes, 3*s.* 6*d.*; ditto two more bears, 1*s.*; bearward, 15*s.*	. . . . . .	0	19	6

In 1599, in the accounts, an item appears of 5*s.* to Mr. Carr, for preaching four sermons a third of the sum they in 1589 give to the bearward, and not as much as they gave two years afterwards, 1601, to the bearward in 'the great cocke fighte.'

The Stage Coach.

Circa 1765.

RESOLVED to visit a far distant friend,
A porter to the *Bull and Gate* I send,
And bid the slave at all events engage
Some place or other in the *Chester* stage.
The slave returns, 'tis done as soon as said,
Your honour's sure when once the money's paid.
My brother whip, impatient of delay,
Puts to at three and swears he cannot stay,
(Four dismal hours ere the break of day)
Roused from sound sleep (thrice called) at length I rise,
Yawning, stretch out my arms, half closed my eyes,
By steps and lanthorn enter the machine
And take my place—how cordially !—between
Two aged matrons of excessive bulk ;
To mend the matter too, of meaner folk :
While in like mode jammed in on t'other side
A bullying captain and a fair one ride,
Foolish as fair, and in her lap a boy,
Our plague eternal, but her only joy.
At last, the glorious number to complete,
Steps in my landlord for that bodkin seat.

When soon by ev'ry hillock, rutt, and stone,
Into each other's face by turns were thrown ;
This granam scolds ; that, coughs ; the captain swears ;
The fair one screams, and has a thousand fears,
While our plump landlord, trained in other lore,
Slumbers at ease, nor yet ashamed to snore ;
And Master *Dicky* in his mother's lap,
Squalling at once brings up three meals of pap.
Sweet company ! next time I do protest, sir,
I'll walk to *Dublin* ere I ride to *Chester*.

Line 14. 'Two aged matrons of excessive bulk.'—This in a ballad about contemporaneous is worded rather stronger :

' Squeezed in 'twixt two bolsters of talkative fat.'

The Death Omen.

A Legend of Blackmere or Brereton's Lake.

'Of neighbours Blackmere named of stranger's Brereton's Lake.'—*Drayton.*

I.

STRUCK down the Lord of *Brereton* lies
Tossing on restless bed ;
'Tis seven days since in vain he tries
To ease his bursting head.

II.

His bloodshot eyes are strange to rest,
His mad pulse wildly throbs ;
Friends grieve, but hide their sorrow, lest
They double his wife's sobs.

III.

Though the leech speaks of hope the word
He knows life's course is run,
He fears, alas ! that *Brereton*'s lord
Won't see another sun.

IV.

The old nurse tearless, sentry sits,
　His ruffled pillow smooths,
Or seeks to cool the fire-parched lips,
　Or damps of death removes.

V.

She's heard men tell her nursling's praise,
　First 'mongst a gallant race ;
He was not one in youthful days
　The old name to disgrace.

VI.

She's seen him bring to these old halls
　A young and noble bride ;
With vassals' welcome rang the walls,
　Oh ! *Brereton* was their pride !

VII.

Again, before twelve months, a roar
　Of joy, and doings rare,
As she midst tenants proudly bore
　Aloft her nursling's heir.

VIII.

But now, alas ! woe worth the day !
　She watched her lord's death-bed ;
Could she of hope but see one ray !
　Could she die in his stead !

IX.

At last, as night steals o'er the plain,
   She can no longer stay ;
Into the darkness hastes amain,
   And hurries far away.

X.

The *Brereton*'s fate, stern she resolves
   From *Brereton*'s lake to learn
The mystery that *Blackmere* solves
   Was now her sole concern.

XI.

She reached the margin of the lake,
   Hushed, hushed, was all around :
Till nature should again awake,
   To watch she sat her down.

XII.

No screech-owl floated on the breeze,
   From distant church-tower strayed ;
No night wind whistled through the trees,
   The moon no ban dog bayed.

XIII.

Naught recked the watching nurse of fear ;
   Of self she had no thought,
But of her lord, to her so dear,
   In cold death's meshes caught.

XIV.

And now the streaks of dawn began
  To cross the eastern sky ;
Then in the lake that watcher wan
  Sought what she might descry.

XV.

The *Mere*, worked as with wintry storm,
  Though all was still around,
And shadows seemed of startling form,
  Through gloaming mists to bound.

XVI.

The black waves surged against the shore,
  Seething with upward throe ;
Strange water-monsters seemed to roar,
  And sport themselves below.

XVII.

Sudden the watcher, pale with care,
  Sprang up like one distressed,
And tossed her shrivelled arms in air,
  And beat her aged breast.

XVIII.

Convulsive sobs, wild scream on scream,
  Ring through the murky air :
Well might a startled listener deem
  Some hellish orgies near !

XIX.

Why looks that watcher like despair ?
  What mean those piercing screams ?
Why toss those withered arms in air ?
  Why so distraught she seems ?

XX.

'Tis that amidst the waves she sees
  (Boiling with wondrous rage),
The blackened trunks of floating trees
  To *Brereton*—death's presage !

XXI.

Slowly the old nurse quits the strand
  Of that dark fatal *Mere* ;
No hope hath she from flood or land,
  The *Brereton*'s time is near.

XXII.

For blackened trunks ne'er rise at all,
  From *Bagmere*'s depths profound ;
But when the head of *Brereton Hall*
  Is doomed to certain death.

The Breretons of Brereton as a Cheshire family are extinct; their lands and their old Hall has past away to the stranger. The Mere (known by the three names mentioned as above, and quoted by Fuller 200 years since, as the only wonder in Cheshire, and specially noticed by Drayton in his 'Polyolbion,' published in 1613) is partially drained and its mysteries vanished. In Sir Philip Sydney's 'Seven Wonders of England,' we find the following :—

> The Breretons have a lake which, when the sun
> Approaching warms (not else), dead logs up sends
> From hideous depth, which tribute when it ends,
> Sore sign it is the lord's last thread is spun.

The Highwayman Outwitted.

I.

T'S of a rich farmer in *Cheshire*,
   To market his daughter did go,
Thinking that nothing would happen her,
   For she'd oftentimes been there before ,
   For she'd oftentimes been there before.

II.

She met with a lusty highwayman,
   A pistol he placed to her breast,
Crying, ' Give me thy money and clothing,
   Or else thou shalt die in distress ;
   Or else thou shalt die in distress.'

III.

He hipped her and stripped her stark naked,
   And gave her the bridle to hold,
And there she stood shivering and shaking,
   Almost starving to death in the cold ;
   Almost starving to death in the cold.

IV.

She placed her right foot in the stirrup,
    And mounted his horse like a man ;
Over hedges and ditches she galloped,
    Crying, ' Catch me thou rogue if thou can ; '
    Crying, ' Catch me thou rogue if thou can.'

V.

' Oh daughter ! oh daughter ! what's kept thee,
    What's kept thee so long at the taan ? '
' Oh father ! I've been in much danger,
    But the rogue he has done me no harm ;
    But the rogue he has done me no harm.'

The farmer's daughter must have been a good horsewoman, for she appears by the line,

' She placed her right foot in the stirrup,'

to have mounted on the off side.

' To have anyone on the hip' is to have the advantage of anyone, which, I conclude, is the meaning of ' He hipped her.' It appears some, if not many, of the stanzas in this song are lost. In Ingledew's ' Ballads of Yorkshire,' we find the same plot running through ' The Crafty Ploughboy.' The boy had sold a cow, the proceeds of which a highwayman, who had given him a mount, demands from him. The boy throws the money down on the ground, and whilst the highwayman is collecting it, the ploughboy takes advantage of the opportunity and gallops off home. The ballad ends thus :

The master he came to the door, and said thus :
' What the deuce ! has my cow turned into a horse ? '
' Oh no canny master, your cow I have sold,
But was robbed on the road by a highwayman bold.

My money I strewed all about on the ground,
For to take it up the rogue lighted down ;
And whilst he was popping it into his purse,
To make him amends I came off with his horse.'

The master he laughed till his sides he had to hold,
He says, ' For a boy thou hast been very bold ;
And as for the villain thou hast served him right
Thou hast put upon him a clean Yorkshire bite.'

He then searched his bags and quickly he told
Two hundred pounds in silver and gold,
And two brace of pistols.   The lad said ' I vow
I think canny master I've sold well your cow.'

Then the boy for his courage and valour so rare
Three parts of the money he had for his share.
Now, since the highwayman has lost all his store,
He may go a robbing until he gets more.

Miss *Weaver*.

I.

LET *Germany* boast of her beautiful *Rhine*,
    We think more of Miss *Weaver's Rhino*,
And scorn e'en the best of *Johannisburgh* wine,
    Whilst we cling to Miss *Weaver* and Brine oh !

II.

We, do not, like *Germany* go to the *Bad*,
    Sitting round gambling tables so green ;
Nor hard up like boys do we run to our dad,
    But we trust to Miss *Weaver* our queen.

III.

Whilst *banks* all around us may break and be stopt,
    And everywhere panic is seen ;
One bank will ne'er burst, and will ne'er be found propt,
    'Tis the *bank* of Miss *Weaver* I mean.

IV.

Though, perchance, her cellar may not boast of wine,
    Yet nowhere will you find a poor fellow,
For whom, on his table when going to dine,
    Miss *Weaver* don't fill a *saltcellar*.

V.

Of salt she warns everyone not to be chary,
  For her treasures pour forth from *Brine* all ;
No sea-nymph is she, her name is not *Mare*,
  I've ne'er heard she was e'en christened *Sal.*

VI.

Yet we trust she may ne'er *Salvolatile* rove,
  To new regions far off and unknown ;
But constant to *Cheshire* fidelity prove,
  And love *Cheshire*, her sweetheart alone.

VII.

As rivers by nature all haste to their seas,
  So clings she to her own *de la mere*,
And whilst he lives by with his corps of trustees,
  She no danger nor bale need to fear.

VIII.

Our own river-nymph ! 'tis she *liquid*ates bills,
  Our courts, rears, asylum, and bridges,
Through her we escape all the various ills
  With which others county rate fridges.

IX.

Seventy-two stinks to hide (see *Coleridge*), *Cologne*,
  That sweet *eau* distils of *Farina* !
But a four with four *os* each year makes our own,
  Miss *Weaver*—how can we resign her ?

X.

Some talked of her *sale*, we'll trust 'twas but a *sel*,
  Her loss would break the palatine heart ;
No *Mersey* salt knaves shall elope with our belle ;
  From Miss *Weaver* we never will part.

XI.

Bold *Robinhood*'s shire swears by *Nottingham* ale,
  As the foaming stream forth her sons pour ;
But grateful for Miss *Weaver*'s gifts I'll go bail,
  Cheshire cries out, Αριϛον ὑδωρ !

XII.

Let boors swizzle their *hale*, for us θειος Ἁλς
  Hath charms irresistibly greater,
Which hides in its rock home till Miss *Weaver* calls,
  To bear it away on her water.

XIII.

' You should first eat a peck of *salt* ' (so the Dutch say),
  With a man whom you wish for your friend ;
In her argosies Miss *Weaver* carries away
  Enough salt the world's quarrels to end.

XIV.

On the subject of *Paris* the French are *in Seine*,
  So we, when Miss *Weaver* we mention,
Should anyone venture our heiress to blame,
  We should at once spring to attention !

XV.

Our sweetheart hath the true philosopher's stone,
    That sages in vain have sought after ;
She turns salt to gold by her power alone,
    Wherever the billows may waft her.

XVI.

Her watermark vainly may forgers pursue,
    They are foiled in their wiles and their crafts;
But still she gives *honour* where honour is due ;
    Only see how she *honours* our *drafts*.

XVII.

Men formed of mud are, so anatomists say,
    For less noble mankind is than she :
Miss *Weaver's* fair shape was not moulded in clay,
    Her motto ' *excelsior* ' must be.

XVIII.

Let each *Cheshire* man his own maiden select,
    Whom he would crown queen of our *witches*,
Where with grace and beauty so many are deckt,
    Of choice the great nicety, sich is.

XIX.

But crown of our *wyches*, one only dare claim,
    'Tis Miss *Weaver's*, Miss *Weaver's* alone :
For ever she facile princess shall reign,
    Sparkling bright on her salt crystal throne.

T

XX.

This queen of all river-nymphs, such is our boast,
   Had both welcomed and married the *Dane*,
Long before *Alexandra* had come to our coasts,
   Like her *Chester*'s earl hath done the same.

XXI.

Here's a health to Miss *Weaver !* a goblet fill up,
   A full brimmer of old ruby wine.
Should one *Cheshire* renegade pass by the cup,
   He shall drain a full bumper of brine.

The river Weever rises in the county, and never leaves it till it falls into the Mersey :

' His fountain and his fall both Chester's rightly born.'

It joins the river Dane at Davenham. In 1720 the Act for making it navigable was first past. Since that period it has produced a very large revenue, which is spent to the advantage of the county.

Lord Delamere is the present chairman of the Weever.

Cheshire May Song.

[Copied for me from memory by George Leigh of Lymm, not unlike one I have already copied from Halliwell's Palatine Anthology. It is the song now sung in the Lymm district.]

I.

LL on this pleasant evening together cometh we,
    For the summer springs, so fresh, green, and gay,
To tell you of a blossom that buds on every tree,
    Drawing near to the merry month of May.

II.

Rise up, the master of this house, all in your chain of gold,
    For the summer springs, so fresh, green, and gay ;
We hope you will not be offended, this night we make so bold,
    Drawing near the pleasant month of May.

III.

Oh! rise, the mistress of this house, with gold upon your breast,
    For the summer springs, so fresh, green, and gay ;
And if your body be asleep, we hope your soul's at rest,
    Drawing near to the merry month of May.

IV.

Sweet *Flora*, in her prime, down by yon river see,
   Where the fields and the meadows look gay ;
Where the little birds are singing, sweet flowers are springing,
   And the summer springs, so fresh, green, and gay.

V.

He hanged on a tree our *Saviour* to be,
   And so did our *Lord God* provide
To clothe and to feed our bodily need,
   And to save our souls when we die.

VI.

Now again comes the spring, which causes us to sing,
   And every living creature to rejoice,
For giving thanks to Him that sends us everything
   That is needful for man and for beast.

VII.

Oh! this is pleasant, singing sweet flowers they are springing,
   And the summer springs, so fresh, green, and gay ;
Right happy are those people who in their hearts give thanks,
   Full and still, to their great *Lord* alway.

VIII.

God bless your house and company, your riches and your store,
   For the summer springs, so fresh, green, and gay,
And all within your gates we wish you ten times more,
   Drawing near to the merry month of May.

IX.

In the midst of peace and plenty we wish to leave you here,
    For the summer springs, so fresh, green, and gay.
We will come no more a singing until another year,
    Drawing near to the merry month of May.

A Legend of *Rostherne* Mere.

I.

ERRILY, merrily rang the bells,
    The bells o'er *Rostherne* mere,
The tale of joy their soft echo tells
    E'en *Bowden* heights may hear.

II.

At *Rostherne* church long, long ago,
    Repairs some workmen make,
When, as they laboured cheerily oh,
    They felt the tower shake.

III.

As the tower shook, the largest bell
    Was riven from its place,
And eke loud clattering down it fell,
    And rolling 'gan apace.

IV.

Down the steep cliff-like bank it rolled
    That frowns above the mere,
Through the fragrant birch and lindens old,
    At length the lake drew near.

LEGEND OF ROSTHERNE MERE.

V.

It stopped at the brink ; hard strove the men
    To force it up the crag,
Back to the tower to strain again
    Oh 'twas a weary drag !

VI.

A sulky labourer madly cried,
    ' Oh, would the Devil had you ! '
But scarce he'd spoke when the bell belied
    To the wave downwards flew.

VII.

But first in its headlong course it crushed
    Th' unlucky wight who swore,
Then down the wild crag madly rushed ;
    They never saw it more.

VIII.

Sunk in the depths of that mere profound
    To which there's bottom none,
And as it sank a dull gurgling sound
    Just to the surface won.

IX.

Now sadly, oh ! sadly moans the peal,
    And mourns that fatal hour;
They seem o'er the bell to ring a knell
    That fell from *Rostherne* tower.

The Iron Gates.

A Legend of Alderley.

I.

LOVE those tales of ancientry,
  Those tales to fancy true,
That bring things back from fairyland
  In all their glittering hue.
I love to hear of stalwart knights,
  Of squires, and dwarfs, and fays,
Whose gambols in the pale moonlight
  Fill rustics with amaze.
Those things are to a musing wight
  Substantial things to view.
    I love those tales of ancientry,
    Those tales to fancy true.

II.

I love those tales my grandame told
  When I sat on her knee,
And looked into her aged face
  With wonder filled and glee ;

Those tales that made me quake with fear,
  Though trembling with delight,
As some huge giant fell to earth
  When vanquished in the fight ;
Or some magician gave his aid
  To whom that aid was due.

III.

Once on a time there was a man,
  A miller he by trade,
Down by yon brook he had his mill,
  Where now the bridge is made :
An honest man that miller was,
  An honest name did own,
His word would pass for forty pounds
  Where'er that name was known ;
And no one doubted what he said,
  For credence was his due.

IV.

The miller had a noble horse,
  It was an iron-grey;
It had a flowing mane and tail,
  And pranced in spirit gay ;
It looked like to a warrior's steed
  Its bearing was so good :
And much the miller prized his horse,
  And boasted of his blood.
He rode him hard, but fed him well,
  And he was sleek to view.

V.

The miller to the market went
　All on a market day,
And, as his custom always was,
　Bestrode his gallant grey ;
He bought and sold and profit made,
　And added to his store.
Then homeward went along the road
　He oft had gone before.
But his good steed and he must part,
　Though grievous the adieu.

VI.

His way lay o'er a barren heath,
　Where now are farms and fields,
For land where naught but thistles grew
　Now wheat and barley yields ;
The time was toward the gloaming hour,
　When things are dimly seen ;
No house nor man was in his sight,
　It was a lonely scene.
His horse springs sideways with a start !
　The thing is something new.

VII.

The grey horse made a sudden start,
　The miller in amaze
Looked out, and in the twilight gloom
　An ancient met his gaze ;

An ancient man there stood to view
  Where just before was none ;
His horse stood still, and he himself
  Felt rooted like a stone.
That aged man the silence broke :
  The horse did start anew.

VIII.

The man was clad like to a monk,
  A reverend air had he ;
A white beard floated from his chin,
  He wore a rosary.
He stretched his hand (ere yet he spoke),
  A hand of skin and bone ;
(The goodly grey seemed reft of power,
  And seemed to turn to stone).
Mildly he on the miller looked,
  The miller powerless too.

IX.

' I want thy horse, sell me thy horse,
  That good and gallant steed ;
I'll give thee gold to fill thy purse,
  For much thy horse I need.'
So spoke that old mysterious monk.
  The miller quoth he, ' Nay,
I would be loath to sell my horse,
  My good, my gallant grey :
For if I should my grey horse sell,
  I might the bargain rue.'

X.

'I want thy horse, sell me thy horse,'
  Again that old monk said
'Name but the price, whate'er it be
  It quickly shall be paid.
But certes 'tis, thy horse and thee
  Must part within the hour.
Take gold whilst gold thou mayst receive,
  And whilst to give I've power.'
The miller heaved a bitter sigh,
  The grey horse trembled too.

XI.

'I want thy horse, sell me thy horse,'
  A third time spoke the man ;
'Again I say I'll give thy price ;
  Then yield him whilst thou can ;
For I have power to make him mine
  Despite what thou mayst say,
But good King *Arthur* told me first
  To ask thy price and pay :
It is for him I want thy horse,
  And gold I bid in lieu.

XII.

'For good King *Arthur* did not die,
  As idle tales have said,
And years and years must pass away
  Ere he sleeps with the dead.

For *Merlin* from the battle bore
  His friend and King away,
That he might lead his chivalry
  In *England*'s needful day :
It is for him I want thy steed ;
  Then yield thy King his due.'

XIII.

There was a magic in his voice
  That charmed, yet filled with fear,
And made his words fall like commands
  Upon the listener's ear.
An impulse by his voice was given,
  Which no man might gainsay.
The miller said he'd sell his horse,
  He heard but to obey.
' Then follow me,' the old monk said,
  ' And I will pay thy due.'

XIV.

The monk strode right across the heath,
  The miller followed too ;
Till they came to a green hillside
  With an iron gate in view.
The miller knew the country well,
  Each rock, each brake, each dell,
But could not in his mem'ry trace
  The portal of that hill.
The monk bade ope the Iron Gate,
  And open wide it flew.

xv.

The monk led through that Iron Gate,
    The miller past likewise;
They scarce were through, it sudden closed
    With loud and thundering noise ;
And whilst they were within the hill
    A strange mysterious light
Shone all around, and still revealed
    Each wonder to the sight ;
And much the miller was amazed
    At all that met his view.

xvi.

For first the monk the miller led
    To cavern large and wide,
In which lay twice ten thousand men,
    All sleeping side by side ;
And they were cased in armour all
    Of purest steel so bright,
And each man's falchion near him lay
    All ready for the fight ;
And shield and lance each warrior had
    Ready disposed in view.

xvii.

And as the monk passed slowly on,
    Each warrior turned him o'er,
Awoke a moment from their sleep,
    Then sank down as before.

'It is not time ! it is not time !'
　The old monk calmly said,
'And till the time is perfected
　This rock must be thy bed ;
For ye are for a noble work,
　And are a noble crew.'

XVIII.

Then to the miller turning round,
　He said with accents bland,
'These are King *Arthur*'s chivalry,
　The noblest in the land !
Each warrior stretched before thee now
　Hath been well tried in fight,
And proved himself before the foe
　To be a valiant knight ;
By *Merlin*'s power all here are laid,
　But will go forth anew.

XIX.

'When *England*'s troubles painful grow,
　And foemen cause her grief,
Then *Arthur* and his noble knights
　Will haste to her relief ;
And then with deeds of chivalry
　All *England* will resound ;
And none so worthy as these knights
　Will in the land be found ;
For they are *England*'s paladins,
　Men great and gallant too.'

XX.

Then onwards to another cave
　The old monk led the way,
Where twice ten thousand gallant steeds
　Were slumbering time away,
And by each horse a serving man.
　It was a noble sight,
To see that band of gallant steeds
　All harnessed for the fight !
And when the miller's horse came there
　He fell and slumbered too.

XXI.

' Your horse is mine,' the old man said ;
　' A noble price I'll pay ;
Thou seest he's mine, for now thou canst
　Not move him hence away ;
He'll good King *Arthur*'s war steed be,
　And bear him bravely forth :
When thy head, honest miller,
　Forgets all things on earth,
By *Merlin* he preserved will be,
　As now he is to view.'

XXII.

Then forth the old monk led the way
　To a cave of smaller size :
But who may tell the sight that met
　The miller's wond'ring eyes !

A glowing light that cave contained,
  Which fell on stone and gem ;
And they threw back that glowing light
  As all too mean for them ;
And sparkling shone that glittering cave
  With stones of every hue.

XXIII.

And there the miller saw huge heaps
  Of gold in coin and ore.
The monk he bade the miller take
  His horse's price and more.
' Take what thou wilt, take what thou canst,
  I stint thee not,' saith he ;
The miller thought of his tolling dish,
  And helped himself right free :
He took such store of gems and gold
  To walk he'd much ado.

XXIV.

The monk then led him forth the hill
  To th' open heath again,
And said, ' Thou art a favoured man
  Within that hill to have been.
'Tis but to some few mortals given
  To see that iron door ;
And once thy back is to it turned
  Thou 'lt see it there no more.
In peace pass on—thy way lies there :
  I bid thee, friend, Adieu.'

XXV.

The miller looked, the monk was gone,
　And he stood there alone,
And turning toward the Iron Gate,
　Saw but the hill of stone.
The miller lived a prosperous man,
　And long dwelt at the mill,
And oft to seek the Iron Gate
　He wandered towards the hill;
But never more that gate he saw,
　For aye it shunned his view.

XXVI.

And it was said that wizard monk
　Had told him wondrous things,
Of all that must to *England* hap
　Through a long line of kings;
Had made him wise beyond all men.
　And certes he looked grave,
When asked what things the monk revealed,
　Or what reward he gave;
But years, long years have past and gone
　Since he gave death his due.

XXVII.

And since his death full many a man
　Has sought that Iron Gate,
And wandered near that grey hillside
　At early morn and late;

But still the gate is kept from view,
  By *Merlin* watched each hour,
And will till off King *Arthur* rides
  With all his knightly power ;
But no one knows when that may be.
  My tale is told—Adieu.

XXVIII.

Such was the tale my grandame told
  Whilst I sat on her knee,
And looked into her aged face
  With wonder filled and glee ;
And such a tale I loved to hear,
  And listen yet I can ;
For oft what has beguiled the child
  Will still beguile the man :
Those things are to a musing wight
  Substantial things to view.
      I love those tales of ancientry,
      Those tales to fancy true.

The *Downes'* Blast.

I.

LOUD echo shouts back as the sound sweeps past
    The *Downes'* old feudal rights,
As on Midsummer's day he blows a blast
    On bleak *Windgather's* heights.

II.

He holds his lands by the blast of the horn,
    And who dare say him nay?
If *Windgather's* heights on Midsummer's morn
    Resound the bugle's lay.

III.

The murderer shrinks as he hears the call,
    He knows if caught redhand,
That in *Gallows Yard* at *Overton* Hall,
    By *Downes'* word he'll be hanged.

IV.

'The stag cowers low in his heathery lair,
    Close midst his bracken bed ;
When the shrill horn at morn rings through the air,
    He hides his antlered head.

V.

Downes' right, for the King is to rouse the deer,
    And whenever he rides, I wisse,
Downes holds the King's stirrup, whilst that proud peer,
    The Lord *Derby*, holds his.

.   .   .   .

VI.

Years follow years, still unchanged as of yore,
    Are stern *Windgather's* heights ;
But on Midsummer's morn the horn never more
    Shall claim the *Downes* his rights.

VII.

No deer on those hills their limbs now brace,
    Nor in lone corries play ;
The red stag is gone, and the stalwart race
    Of *Downes* has past away.

The family of Downes possessed Taxall from the reign of Edward I. to that of James I. The Downes held their 'land by a blast of the horn' on Midsummer's day, standing on the heights of Windgather, and the yearly payment of a peppercorn. The Downes' family, like many others, at a time when 'might was right,' had a power of life and death in their districts, and a place at Overton Hall still called Gallows Yard was the scene of rough justice or injustice, as the case might be. The head of the Downes' family by right attended the King whenever he hunted in his neighbourhood. Lord Derby, instead of absolutely holding Downes' stirrup after Downes had held the King's, is said to have compounded with his dignity by holding a whip or a strap towards the stirrup when Downes mounted. The Overton Hall estate is now owned by the Jodrells of Yeardsley.

The *Verona* Bogart.

THE reader of this title may be curious to know the locality indicated by this foreign-sounding name, in the centre of Cheshire. If on the ordnance map of the county he traverses with his eye the line of road leading from Tarporley to Nantwich, he will find, about two miles before reaching Acton, and near the ancient Watling Street, the name 'Verona.' Upon enquiry on the spot, an antique, quaint-looking house of moderate size would be pointed out on the roadside, that may have been built about the middle of the last century, though since modernised. The writer having property adjoining, has early recollections of tales of mystery connected with this old building, which, moreover, formerly belonged to a relative. It was said that on dark nights a white figure was seen flitting about in a supernatural way; that in those bygone times, which to the present generation seem almost mythical—when the traffic of the country was so largely carried on by the four-horse stage, and when the London mail was daily seen passing and re-passing along this road from London to Chester—on dark winter nights there were sometimes seen spiritlike apparitions near this lone dwelling. A phantom would suddenly jump out from the building near the house upon the mail coach, startling the half-a-sleep passengers, and causing the affrighted horses to fly at the top of their speed. When recovering from the vision, the terrified coachman and guard found that their unearthly companion had vanished. For many years the neighbours feared to pass the house after sunset; and if forced to do so, often saw, or fancied they saw, enough to confirm their worst suspicions—that the place was haunted! When the writer knew the neighbourhood in early life it was inhabited by an elderly lady to whom it belonged, and who with a small household carried on the business of the dairy. In those days, when the cottagers were not so 'high larned' as at present, there was less disposition to question the authenticity of ghost stories, which were pretty current there about. An old tenant one day, whilst relating his experiences, hinted a shrewd suspicion that these ghosts were not altogether immaterial; for that one winter's morning, many years before, he himself set out with his cart to fetch coal from the distant coal-pit, and in passing this same house he saw the veritable Bogart. Feeling in good heart at the time, he approached the figure and challenged it; when, to his surprise, he discovered that it was the landlady herself, who, feeling wakeful and anxious about her cows, had left her bed to look round her farmyard in demi-toilette. The reader may ask, 'How do you account for the affrighted coachman?' It seems almost profane to disturb so interesting a legend; perhaps it might suffice to leave the solution of the enigma to the imagination of our Cheshire gobemouches, guided by such theories as might square with their individual fancies.

If, however, our readers care to hear the explanation volunteered by the present proprietress of the farm, it is as follows: Many years ago an aged woman-servant lived in a part of the building, whose light slumbers were often disturbed by the noisy horn of the mail guard and the heavy tramp of his steeds, and she conceived a design to revenge herself upon her midnight disturbers. She lay in wait till a fitting opportunity, when suddenly, on the rapid passing of the coach, one dark night, she opened her window, and threw a white sheet upon the horses, with what effect we may easily conceive. This explanation seemed to satisfy my informants; but like many another curious myth, we may still feel at liberty to doubt and wonder on. The spirit world truly contains many unsolved enigmas!

As to the origin of the name of this house, I have frequently been at a loss to account for it. 'The two gentlemen of Verona,' make the name familiar to the readers of our national bard; but why give the name to so prosaic a dwelling? though the neighbourhood is not without its poetic associations, for tradition tells of occasional visits of the great lyric poet, our famed Milton—'who married a Cheshire lady'—to Stoke, hard by, and comparatively recently, trees could be pointed out as part of a grove that bore his name. On the ordnance map the name 'Verona' seems to point to another farmhouse adjoining, belonging to the writer; and in his title-deeds it appears that, about a hundred years since, a family of the name of 'Vernon' resided there: this, by a slight change in the letters, might possibly account for the present Italianised name.

We have often heard of immaterial spirits, but the following anecdote seems to point to a new variety of ghosts, which should not pass unnoticed, and may naturally be introduced in this place.

There was and is a house in Staffordshire supposed to be haunted. A gentleman, on his return to the neighbourhood, asked a man whom he knew lived near this house 'How the ghosts were going on?' 'Worser nor ever,' answered the man, 'for they does say as how the ghosses is a breeding.'

E. L.

The Island of the Cross.

A Legend of the Roodeye at Chester.

I.

GES ago, ere the River of *Dee*
    Its natural bounds forsook,—
While it held its own as an arm of the sea,
    And was not a mere languid brook ;

II.

When *Edward* the Elder's progeny reigned
    Secure on their father's throne,
And the *Britons*, of all their lands, retained
    Unconquered *Wales* alone ;

III.

It happened that, watered by *Deva*'s flood
    (So at least says *Saxon* lore),
A primitive Christian temple stood
    On *Haordine*'s sandy shore.

IV.

What prince or martyr lay buried there,
   Or what other saintly spell
May have lent a charm to that house of prayer,
   No record survives to tell.

V.

But this we know,—near its holiest place,
   'Twixt chancel arch and nave,
A stately roodloft, sober grace
   And chastened beauty gave.

VI.

Above, an Image in vestments rich,
   —Fair type of Heaven's Queen,—
Within an ancient sculptured niche,
   Might in those days be seen.

VII.

And poised within her reverend hand
   She held a Cross of wood,
Which the faithful folk of that simple land
   Declared was ' Holy Rood !'

VIII.

Many a pilgrim, too, we're told,
   Came from afar to see
This wondrous relic that had of old
   So blessed the shores of *Dee*.

IX.

That time, on lovely *Montalt*'s height
  There kept strict watch and ward
A warrior noble, *Sitsyllt* hight,
  Penarlag's forest lord!

X.

For why?   Old *Cambria*'s sons at feud
  Were with the *Mercians* then,
And many a conflict had ensued
  Between those vengeful men.

XI.

Nay, though a truce had come, there seemed
  No settled thought of rest,
Hence caution our good *Sitsyllt* deemed
  The safest course and best.

XII.

Thus day and night did *Haordine* spies
  Their round of duty take,
To guard from treachery or surprise
  'The Headland o'er the Lake.'

XIII.

'Twas a scorching summer,—the grass, the grain,
  And other fruits of earth
Had drooped and perished for lack of rain,—
  Then famine came, and dearth !

XIV.

The springs were hushed, and the streamlets dry,—
   ' *Penarlag*, thou'rt wholly undone !
Thy herds lie exhausted, thy little ones cry
   For relief, where alas ! there is none ! '

XV.

But now from her home, in that *Montalt* camp,
   Moved a form of comeliness rare,
Whose grace and presence united to stamp
   Her the fairest of *Haordine*'s fair.

XVI.

Lady *Trawst* was the child of Prince *Elys* the brave,
   And 'twas held, with one common accord,
That ne'er father a lovelier daughter gave
   Than he to *Penarlag*'s lord.

XVII.

But if nature had smiled upon *Sitsylll*'s spouse,—
   That lady of princely blood !—
She had yet higher charms, tradition avows,
   For was she not pious and good ?

XVIII.

Yea, daily at matins and evensong
   Her custom it was to repair
To the church, and prayerfully mingle among
   The small knot of worshippers there.

XIX.

The Lady on that day meekly knelt,
  At that sacred shrine she prayed,
And for all who in *Montalt*'s lordship dwelt
  Implored the *Virgin*'s aid.

XX.

Long time, they say, upon bended knee
  Did Lady *Trawst* remain,
With others in that fair sanctuary,
  Praying aloud for rain.

XXI.

Dark lowered the western setting sun,
  Red lightnings rent the sky,
Whilst booming thunder's clarion
  Rolled ominously by.

XXII.

Louder and nearer grew the shock,
  As that dreadful tempest raged ;
But it found *Penarlag*'s trembling flock
  In earnest prayer engaged.

XXIII.

Another and yet more vivid flash
  Gleams through those sacred walls ;
Then, scarcely heard 'mid that thunder's crash,
  The *Virgin*'s image falls !

XXIV.

One piercing cry ! and 'twas only one,
  For death had triumphed there;
And Lady *Trawst*'s bright soul had flown
  To Him who answers prayer !

XXV.

Loud maddening shrieks now rent the air
  On *Deva*'s Cambrian shore,
And shouts of anger resounded where
  Devotion reigned before.

XXVI.

Down tore those villagers forlorn
  Their Image, now disgraced ;
And twelve men 'good and true' were sworn
  To try the cause in haste.

XXVII.

Hincot of *Hancot, Comberbache,*
  Gill, Pughet, Hughet, Pate,
Leche, Milling, Span of *Mancot, Lache,*
  Peat, Corbin of the Gate.

XXVIII.

These were the jury, and this the court
  Impanelled the plaint to try ;
And their verdict amounted to this, in short,
  That the Image at once must *die!*

XXIX.

But *how*, was the question,—to hang or burn
A relic so highly esteemed,
Was an act of sin, of which they in turn
Appeared to have scarcely dreamed.

XXX.

So, yielding to reason, in some degree,
And binding the Cross to her side,
They laid them both down on the sands of *Dee*,
Within reach of the rising tide.

XXXI.

The moon shone full on that *Montalt* steep,
While *Trawst* was borne to her grave;
And the Holy Rood floated, with surging sweep,
On the crest of that midnight wave.

XXXII.

As the sorrowing mourners left the grave,
And returned to their homes again,
Heaven answered their lost one's prayer, and gave
' The sound of abundance of rain !'

XXXIII.

Next day, for that Virgin and Holy Rood
Each *Montalt* penitent calls;
But both had been left by the ebbing flood
'Neath *Legeceaster*'s walls !

XXXIV.

Though camp and city adjacent were,
　　Yet hatred between them reigned ;
So, where the waters had left them, there
　　Those relics perforce remained.

XXXV.

And there, on the spot where the citizens found
　　That emblem of *Calvary*'s tree,
They raised, on an eye, or islet mound,
　　A stone Cross, pleasant to see.

XXXVI.

In memory, too, of that selfsame day,
　　That marsh,—now green and dry,—
Has ever since borne, as well it may,
　　Its well-known name ROOD-EYE !

HAORDINE.　The original way of spelling Hawarden, Flintshire.

PENARLĀG, or PEN-Y-LLWCH.　The British name of the place, signifying 'The Headland above the Lake.'

MONTALT.　The Norman title of the entire lordship, of which Hawarden was the principal seat.　This title has also, but apparently in error, been given to the neighbouring town of Mold.

SITSYLLT.　Governor of Hawarden Castle, A.D. 946.　Lady Trawst, his wife, was daughter of Elys, son of Anarawd, Prince of Wales.

LEGECEASTER.　The Saxon name of Chester (the City of the Legion).

Old *Mynshull* of *Erdeswick.*

[A Royalist song found amongst the family papers in an old oak chest at Erdeswick Hall, one of the seats of the Minshull family.]

I.

ARISE! and away for the king and y^r land!
Farewell to ye couch and y^r pillow;
With spear in its rest, and with rein in hand,
Let us rush on ye foe like a billow!

II.

Call the hind from ye plough, and ye herd from the fold,
Bid y^r wassiles to take a long pull;
Then ride for old *Erdeswick*, whose banner's unrolled
For the cause of King *Charles* and *Mynshull*.

III.

Ride, ride, with red spur—there is death in delay;
'Tis a race for dear lyfe with y^e *Devil*;
For if *Cromwell* prevail, and ye king now gives way,
Our land must in slavery revel.

IV.

Piers Dutton is up, and young *Brereton* is nigh,
    And *Ffytton* is over yᵉ river ;
From *Gawsworth* to *Vernon* 'One and All !' is the cry,
    And ' the king and old *Mynshull* for ever !'

V.

There was *Leycester*, and *Massey*, and *Poole* of old fame,
    And *Leigh* with his famed triple banner;
Old *Venables* too, with his dragon and flame,
    And *Egerton* from the Old Manor.

VI.

Young *Mainwaring* fell by the side of hys sire,
    Stout *Booth* was revenged for him there ;
For the foe left his grim trunkless head in the myre,
    By the sword of old *Dunham*'s young heir.

VII.

Aye, 'by waif, soc, and theam, you may know *Cheshire* men'
    'Mid the names and the nobles here given ;
But if truth to the king be a signal, why then
    Ye can find out old *Mynshull* in heaven.

VIII.

' By the Crescent and Star my forefathers won
    On the plains of old *Palestine* ;
These Roundheads shall feel the effect of my steel,
    For age has improved it like wine !'

IX.

There was death in each stroke, whilst old *Mynshull* thus
　And Roundheads fell off in a cluster ;　　　　[spake,
Such havoc he made, that his trusty old blade
　Told a tale the next day at their muster.

X.

At *Edgehill* he fought, and at *Worcester* he fell,
　But vain were the visions he cherished ;
For the brave *Cheshire* heart that our king loved so well
　In the grave of y^e *Mynshulls* lyes perished.

XI.

Then ' Hurrah for the king ! ' our *Cheshire* men sing,
　Let the bells give a merrie round peal !
For loyal and true to his church and his king
　Old *Mynshull* for ever did feel.

XII.

May his sons prove as true to their church and their king,
　And act, like their sire, with decision
And firmness whenever the foe's on the wing,
　For from heaven they get their commission!

- - - - - - -

Stanza 7.　' By waif, soc, and theam, you may know Cheshire men.'

Waif. From a Saxon derivation, goods dropped by a thief when pursued ; also goods
and chattels lost, and not claimed for a year and a day, which, after certain forms, become
the property of the lord of the manor.

Soc, soccage. From soc, a ploughshare; in Cheshire, suck. A certain tenure of lands held by inferior husbanding services to be performed to the lord of the fee. This tenure was of two sorts, free soccage and base soccage, otherwise called villanage. Socmen were, in the time of the Saxons, a sort of tenant that manured and tilled the peculiar demesnes of their lord, yielding him work and not rent.

Theam, team. A royalty granted by the king's charter to a lord of a manor for the restraining and judging of bondmen and villains in his court. Many Cheshire families— the Dones, Davenports, &c.—had the right of life and death on their own lands. This is said to be the origin of the Davenport crest—'a rogue's head couped at the shoulders, with a halter round the neck, Or.'

The Synagogue Well.

I.

HE *Roman*, in his toilsome march,
Disdainful viewed this humble spot,
And thought not of *Egeria*'s fount
　　And *Numa*'s grot.

II.

No altar crowned the margin green,
No dedication marked the stone ;
The warrior quaffed the living stream,
　　And hasten'd on.

III.

Then was upreared the *Norman* keep
Where from the vale the uplands swell,
But, unobserved, in crystal jets
　　The waters fell.

IV.

In conquering *Edward*'s reign of pride,
Gay streamed his flag from *Frodsham*'s tower,
But saw no step approach the wild
　　And sylvan bower ;

v.

Till once, when *Mersey*'s silvery tides
Were reddening with the beams of morn,
There stood beside the fountain clear
A man forlorn ;

vi.

And as his weary limbs he laid
In its cool waters, you might trace
That he was of the wandering tribe
Of *Israel*'s race.

vii.

With pious care, to guard the spring,
A masonry compact he made,
And all around its glistening verge
Fresh flowers he laid.

viii.

' *God* of my fathers ! ' he exclaimed,
' Beheld of old in *Horeb*'s mount,
Who gav'st my sires *Bethesda*'s pool
And *Siloa*'s fount ;

ix.

' Whose welcome streams, as erst of yore,
To *Judah*'s pilgrims never fail,
Tho' exiled far from *Jordan*'s banks,
And *Kedron*'s vale ;—

x.

‘ Grant that when yonder frowning walls,
With tower and keep, are crushed and gone,
The stones the *Hebrew* raised may last,
And from his well the strengthening spring
May still flow on ! ’

The Synagogue well, evidently one of great antiquity, and, before an attempt was made to improve it, of most picturesque appearance, is in the grounds at Park Place, Frodsham. The origin of the name ‘ Synagogue Well ’ has occasioned much discussion ; but the tradition respecting it may be considered as embodied in the preceding stanzas. Of Frodsham Castle, which was contiguous to the well, scarcely a vestige remains.

The Old Times of *Cheshire*.

I.

HE old times ! those old days !
　　Some say that they were bad,
But still I think those old days
　　Were anything but sad ;

II.

When the wild cattle now confined
　　Within *Lyme*'s spacious park,
Wandered where'er they had a mind,
　　Through *Maxfield*'s forest dark,

III.

Snuffed the free breeze of *Shutlingslaw*,
　　Or swam the rapid *Dane*,
Or from the grim wolf's blood-stained jaw
　　Rescued their calves again.

IV.

From *Blacon* point to *Hilbree*,
　　Squirrels in search of food
Might then jump straight from tree to tree,
　　So thick the forest stood.

V.

No chimneys tall, with choking smoke
    Obscured the light of day,
No busy noise the silence broke,
    Where now's a crowded way.

VI.

Then met at butts a gallant lot,
    Each township in array ;
And he who the best arrow shot
    Was crowned lord of the day.

VII.

Then banners waved o'er *Beeston*'s wall,
    And clarion sounded loud,
As *Cheshire* sprang to honour's call,
    Cheshire, midst proudest, proud.

VIII.

As minstrel told his warlike tale,
    With shouts the castle rang,
And maidens listened, but turned pale
    As deeds of blood he sang.

IX.

Then bold knights strove for ladies' love,
    Or desperate venture dared ;
Their love and valour could they prove,
    Naught they for danger cared.

X.

I do not say those old days
I wish again we had,
But still I think those old days
Were anything but sad.

' When the wild cattle,' &c.—At Lyme Park is one of the few herds of wild cattle remaining in England.

' From Blacon Point to Hilbree,' &c.—There is an old saying proving the way in which arts of the county, now almost denuded, were once covered with trees:

From Blacon Point to Hilbree
A squirrel may jump from tree to tree.

' Then met at butts,' &c.—In former days, when we won our victories with our bows, law, custom, and inclination made the youth of the county crowd to the shooting butts.

LONDON
PRINTED BY SPOTTISWOODE AND CO
NEW-STREET SQUARE